Needing

ISBN # 978-1-78651-913-9

Cover Art by Posh Gosh ©Copyright 2016

Interior text design by Claire Siemaszkiewicz

Pride Publishing

This is a work of fiction. All characters, places and events are from the author's imagination and should not be confused with fact. Any resemblance to persons, living or dead, events or places is purely coincidental.

Published in 2016 by Pride Publishing, Newland House, The Point, Weaver Road, Lincoln, LN6 3QN, United Kingdom.

Pride Publishing is a subsidiary of Totally Entwined Group Limited.

Printed and bound in Great Britain by Clays Ltd, St Ives plc

1

Voices

NEEDING

SARAH MASTERS

Chapter One

Getting calls from the dead in the middle of the night wasn't Oliver Banks' idea of fun.

He stared down at the body resting in the mulch, the limbs at odd angles. Her blonde hair, splayed against a backdrop of soggy leaves, stood out starkly in the beam of his pencil-slim flashlight. Christ, what kind of people did this to another human being? Crazy bastards, that's who. Oliver had dealt with them before, had gazed down at bodies like this too many times to count, and here he was again, called out by the voices in his head and the unexplainable knowledge that someone had been murdered.

The woman, early thirties he guessed, looked as though she'd been out walking. Mud-encrusted hiking boots covered her feet, one tightly tied, the other undone, laces like rigid, dried-out worm skins. Had the killer been interrupted in taking the boot off? And why the fuck would he have done that anyway?

Oliver sighed. Sometimes it was pointless questioning the idiosyncrasies of the warped. Sometimes they just did things. No reason. Just because. He stared at the woman's jean-covered legs. Mud splatters soiled the denim from the top of her boots to her thighs. Had she run through one of the many boggy areas in this now godforsaken field? Had she tried to get away from the bastard who had done this to her? Oliver hadn't been given any details other than the site and the fact that a dead body was there. He'd hauled his arse out of bed then dressed quickly, stuffing his hair under a beanie hat.

He looked down at his battered Nikes. They'd sunk into

the ground and would leave perfect imprints.

Fuck.

He shifted his gaze back to the woman, whose stomach was exposed, her black T-shirt bunched to just below her breasts. The perfect, taut skin showed the woman had taken care of herself, had maybe visited a gym regularly. What a damn waste of a life. Her jacket, a black windbreaker, the fronts open, would have done nothing to keep off the winter chill. She wasn't wearing a hat or scarf, no gloves either, unless whoever had killed her had taken them away. Another oddity that wouldn't surprise Oliver. Killers took the strangest trophies.

There were no marks on her neck or face, no obvious signs of how she'd been killed. No bruising, no knife wounds, no blood. If it wasn't for her arms and legs clearly being broken, the woman might have appeared to have just fallen down and died. He closed his eyes, aware that morning would be here all too soon, that someone walking their dog might well discover the body. Or not. The recent rains had made this field treacherous, and if she wasn't looked at soon by forensics and another burst of rain occurred, evidence would be washed away. Oliver had turned his ankle when traipsing over the field, a hidden pothole that he'd called all the names under the sun. If anyone *chose* to walk here, they were crazy.

"Were you crazy?" he asked, directing his flashlight beam at the corpse's face. "Or were you brought here?"

Oliver swept an arc of light over the grass either side of the body. Yes, there they were in a patch of exposed mud, the footprints of the victim and also someone else. A larger size, undoubtedly those of a man. And it was always a man, wasn't it? At least it had been in Oliver's experience. The grass was trampled so much in places it had been ripped from the ground. The footprints, prominent in a large muddy swathe, were dotted about, but a mass of them, like two people had stood together and tussled, dominated one area.

"So you put up a fight." Oliver hunkered down and studied the woman's nails. Pristine, acrylic, long. "But it seems you didn't get to scratch him. That's a bit of a shit, isn't it?" He winced at his use of language. "I really ought to curb it, but fuck, it just pops out. See?"

Female laughter echoed inside Oliver's head, delicate and sweet. At last, she'd made contact. He'd been waiting for it, had thought the victim would never break through again, but there she was, giggling.

"What kept you?" Oliver laughed gently, saddened that once again he'd be speaking to someone he'd never get to meet in life. Someone who would never use her body to help express herself. Someone who had been snuffed out just because another human being had decided that would be so. "Fucking arsehole."

The giggle came again, then a sigh. Then a sob.

Shit.

"You see yourself here, right?"

Why did he insist on stating the obvious? Oliver sensed her spirit had just caught up with the recent events. That she'd realised she was dead, left in a field for someone to find or for a wild animal to feast on. Or to rot, never to be seen again, unless you counted bones. Not something anyone envisaged for themselves at the best of times, but there it was. A bold, cold fact of life. Sometimes people got offed and didn't get a decent burial.

"Sorry if you heard my thoughts there. I really need to work on my empathy skills. Work on keeping you out when I'm thinking shit like that." Oliver switched off his flashlight, suddenly unable to look at the body now her spirit was with him. It wasn't just a body anymore but a person, one who was in his mind and would hopefully help him track the killer. "Listen, you can either stay here or find someplace else to be, but if you reach out, I'll be listening. If you want me to help, I can. It's just that…" He glanced at the horizon, obscured by a line of gnarly, leafless trees. "I have to call this in so the cops can get you out of this shitty place. Your body, I mean. You? You're free to go wherever you want, but like I said, if you need me, just reach out."

Oliver slid his flashlight in his jeans back pocket. Fuck, what he'd give to be normal, to have his mind to himself.

"Not gonna happen."

He'd burn his Nikes, buy a new pair. As usual. He hated wearing them again once they'd been worn to a scene.

This damn gig was getting expensive.

With another sigh, he walked across the grass towards his car parked on a verge beside the trees that lined the edge of the field. He'd ring the cops—Detective Langham to be exact—speak with him, then go home, get rid of his shoes, shower, maybe catch a bit more sleep. Or maybe, if he was lucky, the dead woman would contact him and they could get to the real work of finding the son of a bitch who had done this.

In his car, he gunned the engine then switched the heat on, letting the vehicle idle along with his thoughts. Daylight might be imminent, but shit, he had to take a moment to compartmentalise what he'd seen, file away the insignificant and concentrate on the important. The woman had struggled so she had known she was in trouble. Did she know her killer? Oliver cursed. He hadn't thought to *fully* check the area, to see if there were two tracks side by side in the grass leading up to the final resting place, or whether there was just one. Was she followed or with someone? Had she willingly walked with this guy or been forced?

"This is where you come in, love," he muttered, cocking his head, awaiting a response. Nothing. "All right, so you don't want to talk right now. I'm cool with that. You just... Yeah, you just take your sweet damn time. Like we have it to waste."

Oliver clamped his lips closed and shielded his thoughts. The woman didn't need to know Oliver was pissed off as hell at his lack of attention to detail, that he'd failed the woman already with his incompetence. He'd been doing this long enough to know the drill by now. Scope the damn area and find out as much as he could without disturbing the body. Get clues, anything to help him find the sick shit who had done this. Still, she'd made contact again, that was the main thing, and he'd have to be content with that.

He glanced at the rear-view mirror and frowned. Was that another vehicle back there? Turning in his seat, he stared out of the back window. It was hard to tell whether it was a car or just a dark mound, a part of the verge. He hadn't taken any notice when he'd arrived, hadn't bloody concentrated *again*. What was up with him tonight? Okay, he hadn't had much sleep, but usually he was a damn sight more alert when called out like this.

A light flickered, right about where a windshield would be, and Oliver's stomach muscles bunched. Was that an interior light going on then off? Had someone struck a match or lighter? He waited, breath held, for the light to appear again. His car engine hummed, the sound of it making him want to get the fuck out of there and back home. If someone was out there, he didn't fancy meeting with them. No. He alerted the police and helped them track the killer. He didn't interact with the insane motherfuckers — not if he could help it.

"But it doesn't always work out like that, does it?"

No, it didn't, but he sure as shit wasn't going to encourage coming face to face with someone who had just killed. Or anyone in this area in the middle of the night. Besides, it wasn't a car. The shape wasn't right. It was a hill. Or something.

A shiver went down his back and the hairs on his neck stood on end.

"Who are you trying to kid? Someone's back there. Someone saw you."

He gritted his teeth and pulled out his phone. Seemed he did this too often lately. The calls from the dead were becoming more frequent, and as soon as one case was solved and closed another came along. He dialled a number he knew by heart and waited for the pick-up.

"Langham."

The strong male voice flipped his stomach.

"Uh, it's me."

A sigh, then, "All right. What have you got?"

"Dead body."

"Now there's a surprise. Where?"

"The field on the Keach Road turnoff. Female. About thirty."

"Right." Another sigh. "Wait for me there."

"I can't."

"Why the hell not?" Langham was getting testy. Not a good thing.

"Because there's a car parked a way behind me."

"Jesus fucking Christ, Oliver! Would you just *stop* visiting the damn sites? Just ring me when you get the information."

"I can't help it. I have to visit. It's how I connect. How I get the bloody information that helps *you* break the case and makes *you* look like a damn superstar."

"Fuck you."

"Backatcha. So, you coming out here or what?"

"I'd like to say 'or what' but—"

"Look, do I wait here or go home?"

"Wait. See if the car moves."

"And if it does? You want me to follow it?"

"Fuck, no! Just take the damn licence plate."

"Right. You staying on the line? You want some company while you get yourself out of bed?"

"I'm already out of bed, already dressed. I'm just getting in my car."

"Well, aren't you just on the fucking ball?"

"Your language, Oliver, is disgusting."

"Yeah, yeah. Deal with it." He looked in the rear-view mirror again. The light flickered once more and headlights burst into life. His guts twisted. "Um, Langham?"

"What?"

"The car's ready to roll."

"Shit. I'm ten minutes away. Get the licence plate."

"But what if it isn't headed my way? It's still back there, just the headlights on. What if it goes the other way?" The car nosed onto the road. "Uh, scrub that. It's heading towards me."

"Good, sit tight."

"No can do. I mean, it's heading *towards* me. *For* me."

"Then get the hell out of there, man!"

Oliver wedged the phone between his shoulder and ear and eased onto the rain-slicked road, headlamps on low beam, their rapiers of light cutting into the darkness. A quick glance in the mirror told him the car was gaining on him at speed. He accelerated, hoping to make it to a farmhouse standing in the distance. It had lights on, creamy squares of hominess that called to Oliver, made him want a normal life with a family that gave a shit whether he lived and breathed. His? They'd cast him out the minute he'd hit eighteen, telling him never to bring his weird arse back because he wasn't right in the head. Yeah, well, they ought to try living like he had for as far back as he could remember. Having dead people in his bloody head, asking for help, taking him places he'd never thought he'd go. Seeing things he'd never thought he'd see. Having mad people follow him in their cars in the middle of the sodding night.

"Don't even go there," he snapped, pushing his foot down on the accelerator. "Too much thought makes Oliver a cranky bastard. Being followed by a possible killer makes Oliver a frightened bastard."

"You talking to me, the victim, or yourself?" Langham asked.

"Myself. Nothing unusual. Nothing to fret about."

"Right. Give me an update."

"Whoever it is…well, let's just say I think they know I've seen them. They're right up my arse. I'm heading west. Farmhouse ahead. The road bends, leads to —"

"Crooks Lane. Yeah, I know where you are."

13

"Didn't anyone ever tell you interrupting was *rude?*"

"Didn't anyone ever tell you you're an infuriating man-bitch?"

He laughed quietly. It helped to calm his taut nerves and adrenaline-fuelled blood. "Yeah, plenty, but never by anyone I gave a shit about." Damn. He hadn't meant to say that. Shit, fuck and damn. "And that was fear talking."

"You're scared?"

"Hell yeah! I'm human. It's natural when being chased by someone. You ought to try the feeling on for size sometime. It's a good thrill."

"Much as I'm enjoying this interaction, Oliver, we'll have to continue it some other time. I've just turned onto Keach. Couple of minutes away. Road's long. Uniforms will be here in a bit, but not in time to deal with this fucker. What's going on?"

He eyed the mirror. "The car's *right* up my arse."

"Uncomfortable."

"Very fucking funny."

"The farmhouse?"

"Still too far away."

A smack to the back of Oliver's car had him shunting forward.

"Shit! *Shit!*"

"What? What's happening, man?"

"He's bumped my tail."

"Well, drive faster!"

Oliver shook his head and stomped on the accelerator, irked that, like him, Langham had a habit of stating the obvious. Maybe that was why they got along—after a fashion. He pelted down the road, creating space between his car and the other. Adrenaline flowed faster, and he coached himself calmer, only to have his nerves jangle as the car pulled across the road and sped up, riding alongside him.

"He's beside me, Langham."

"Yeah, I see that. I'm a good way back, but I see your tail

14

lights."

"Well, drive faster!" he mimicked, smirking despite his fear.

Oliver glanced sideward. The driver stared at him.

"Um, Langham?"

"Yep?"

"You know I said *he'd* bumped my tail?"

"Yeah…"

"Make that a she."

"What?"

"Yeah. Some chick. Black hair. Either that or it's an effeminate man."

"Don't joke about it. Stranger things have happened."

"Don't I know it."

The other car suddenly slewed towards Oliver's car, the side of it crashing into his. He tightened his grip on the steering wheel and focused on the road ahead, driving faster in an attempt to get away.

"Shit," Langham said.

A siren split the air, and a blue strobe of light illuminated the interior of Oliver's car. He looked at the other driver, the woman's face clearer now. Her hands clearer—great big hands that had no business being on a female. After checking the road ahead, Oliver stared back at the car.

"It's a damn mask," Oliver said. "The driver's wearing a damn mask and wig."

"Yeah, and that driver's going to be moving pretty fast away from me any…second…now."

The driver didn't. The car crashed into Oliver's again, an almighty whack that jolted Oliver across the road and onto the verge. The uneven ground beneath his tyres made for a bumpy ride, and he struggled to control his vehicle. Panic threatened to overtake, and he fought to remain alert, on target.

"Oliver, watch yourself."

"I'm trying!"

"There's a damn tree ahead. Move over. Now!"

"I can't! Can't you see the other car's stopping me?" *Oh, fuck. Get me out of here. Please, just get me out of here safe.*

The tree loomed up ahead, and Oliver yanked the wheel, hoping to make it past the wide trunk in time. He did, but his front tyre clipped an exposed root and his car overturned, rattling his teeth and bones. His head smacked the side window, dislodging his phone, and he held back a string of curses. The car kept on rolling, and he heard Langham's voice, tinny and distant, coming out of his phone, wherever the hell it had fallen.

"Follow her!" Oliver shouted. "Or him. Don't worry about me. Just go!"

His car came to a lurching stop. Upside down. He hung, hands still on the wheel, heart beating like a bitch with a score to settle. And shit, he had a score to settle now. Not only did he have a killer to catch, but someone who had also tried to kill him—*and* pissed him off into the bargain.

When his car had spun, he'd felt one of his fingers break.

And *that* was enough to make him see red.

Chapter Two

No one broke his finger and got away with it.

Oliver grimaced. Not only had it broken, but the nail had been ripped off way below the level of acceptability. Fuck, did his fingertip hurt. His temple throbbed. Hitting it on a window would do that, but shit, it felt like he had a lump the size of a damn egg beside his eye.

Assessing his situation, he glanced around and sniffed. It didn't smell like any petrol had leaked, but he wasn't hanging around long enough to find out. Hanging. And he was, still, held in place by his seatbelt. He unclipped it, bracing for another bang to the head as he dropped to the ceiling. Annoyed beyond reasoning, he reached for the door and fumbled with the lock, expecting fate to have played games with him and trapped him inside. Thankfully, the door opened, just not enough for him to climb out. He was slim, but a size below small he was not. Even in his wildest dreams he wouldn't fit through that gap.

With anger and frustration simmering, he clambered across the passenger seat and opened that door. It swung wide with a groan from the hinges, then a pair of legs appeared. He tensed until he spotted a pair of familiar brown loafers.

"I told you to follow the damn driver," Oliver snarled, craning his neck to get a look at Langham.

Langham stared down at him, a tousle-headed blond with a face that showed no signs that he'd been woken out of a deep sleep. Bastard. He did wear a frown, though, which was something. If he hadn't expressed some kind of worry at Oliver's predicament, he'd have gladly blamed him for the broken finger and taken all his irritation out on him. Someone had to pay. Might as well be Langham.

"The uniforms are on it. Do you want some help getting out, or will my offer end with a tirade from your foul mouth and a kick to my shins?"

Oliver almost laughed. Almost. Langham knew him too well. "I'll try and get out myself, and if I can't, *then* you can help me."

"Stubborn bitch."

"That's me. Glad to know someone on this planet digs me." Oliver scrabbled out on hands and knees, the grass cold and wet, soaking through his jeans. He stood and brushed himself off, ignoring the lightheadedness and the throb of his finger. "So, please tell me the other coppers are covering that arsehole."

"Yeah." Langham scrubbed his chin, the rasp of his stubble loud despite Oliver's car engine still growling. "Got the licence number. Good job I did, seeing as *you* didn't."

Oliver widened his eyes. "You had better be joking."

Langham laughed, the sound rich and so infuriating Oliver had the urge to smack him across the face.

"Yeah, I'm joking. Lighten up. Anyone would think you'd just had a car accident."

Oliver walked away, leaving *him* to switch off the engine. *Let him blow himself up.* Langham riled Oliver as often as he could, and most times he could handle it, gave as good as Langham gave him, but now? Here? No, this wasn't fucking funny. He'd find the person who'd made him break a finger if it bloody killed him.

"And maybe it will," he muttered. "Who the hell knows?" Looking over his shoulder he called, "And get my phone, will you?"

He climbed up the embankment, finding himself at the side of the road where he'd veered off course. He had been so close to the farmhouse. So close to not having a boiled egg on his noggin. Lifting his hand, he touched his temple, careful in his exploration. The last thing he needed was pain. He didn't bear it well. It felt as though he had a simple contusion, one that would shrink within a couple of days, and they always felt bigger than they were. Time for vanity later, when he was home safe and a mirror could shock him shitless.

His engine died, and Langham came up behind him. He took his elbow and turned Oliver to face him. His frown was back. Good.

"This is why I ask you not to visit sites, Oliver." He pushed a stray tress of hair back under Oliver's hat. "It's too dangerous."

"Yeah, well." The concern in Langham's eyes pleased Oliver. He'd done just what the hell he'd wanted yet again and in the process had upset Langham. He had to stop that, but when the calls from the dead came, he felt compelled to go and find their bodies. Something he couldn't ignore — he'd tried it and failed several times. "We've been through this before. I can't not come. You don't understand."

"I do, I really do." He took Oliver's hands in his. "But you got hurt this time, and I warned you something like this would happen."

"Yep, but it's done now. No point going on about it." He smiled to ease the acid in his tone. "So, what next?"

"I do what I do, you do what you do. Follow the pattern. It's never failed in the past."

"Right. Well. Uh, could I get a lift home?" Oliver had the urge to do something he'd only thought about previously — to lean forward to kiss him. Instead, he turned away to walk towards his car. "It's a long walk, and I'm fucked if I have the energy to make it."

"You need a doctor first, Oliver." Langham placed Oliver's phone in his hand.

"No thanks. And thanks for getting my phone." He climbed inside and settled in the passenger seat, staring down the embankment at his trusty little Fiat that wasn't so damn trusty anymore. Christ knew how much it would cost to get it fixed.

Langham joined him, starting the engine. "I can't take you back just yet, though."

"Oh. Yeah."

"I need to get to the murder site, maybe get another officer to take you home when they arrive. You'll have questions to answer before that, though. You know the drill."

"Yeah. Good job they know I'm a whacko who can be trusted. That my word is good. Otherwise... Shit, I'm not even going there."

"Best you don't."

Langham drove down the road in silence, leaving Oliver to work out exactly what he was going to say in his statement. The police knew what he did, what he was, and at first had suspected *him* of killing all those people. He could see how they'd arrived at that conclusion, him always knowing where the bodies were, but when he'd given them information the victims had told *him*, leading them to the perpetrators, and had proven alibis, he'd been let off the hook. So to speak. Now they approached him for help, but it didn't work like that. He couldn't just summon the dead and bombard them with questions. He had to be contacted by them, and sometimes the dead just didn't want to speak.

Once, he'd been taken down into the morgue to try to get information from an old guy who'd been found stabbed to death in his home. The grey-haired fella hadn't been in the mood for conversing, had told Oliver straight out to fuck off and mind his own business, and he had. Gladly. He never had been good with the elderly.

Langham pulled over, parking close to where Oliver had earlier. Another shiver abseiled down his spine and he took a moment to wonder whether it was the return to the scene that spooked him or whether the victim teetered on contacting him. He concentrated, sensing nothing but his own thoughts inside his mind, and shrugged. The woman would speak when she felt like it and not before.

Langham cut the engine. "You ready to show me where she is?"

"Yeah."

They strode across the field, Oliver watching out for potholes. He contemplated telling Langham to do the same, but seeing him fall arse over tit was an amusing concept. Oliver led the way, seeing the shape of the body more clearly now the sky had lightened a little. Not much, but enough to show her whereabouts. Oliver stopped in the same place as before and stared at her. Something was different. He narrowed his eyes and reached into his back pocket, relieved his flashlight was still there. Switching it on, he aimed the beam at the woman's T-shirt. It had been clean before. Just a black T-shirt. Now, what appeared to be sugar strands peppered the fabric, the kind that were sprinkled on iced doughnuts. What the fuck? Surely not.

"Um, they weren't here before." He nodded at the multicoloured strands.

"What weren't?"

"The sugar strands. On her T-shirt. Fuck." It dawned on him that someone had been here as he'd walked across the field to his car. It had to have been the person in that other car. Had it been parked there when he'd arrived and he just hadn't seen it? "I'd swear that car wasn't here when I arrived, but now I'm not so sure."

"It might not have been."

Oliver turned to face Langham. "What, it might have come along after I got here?"

"Yep. How long were you here?"

"A while. Half an hour?"

"Right. Maybe the killer forgot to put those strands on her and came back. No maybe about it—it's obvious that's what happened. What did you do when you got in your car?"

"I switched on the engine and had a little think."

"A little think. Right. How long for?"

Oliver tried to estimate the time. "I don't know. Five minutes maybe?"

"And you noticed the car when?"

"I turned on the engine, glanced in the mirror."

"Okay. Then what?"

"I saw a light."

"Which could have been...?"

"The driver getting back in the car. Shit."

"Yes, shit. You were lucky he didn't bloody come for you. So, in future, will you at least ring me and let me know you're going to a site, and wait for me to go with you?"

Oliver nodded. Yeah, he was a stubborn bitch, liked to think he didn't need any help and could handle himself, but the past hour or so had been an eye-opener. Langham was right. He shouldn't be doing this crap alone.

"Good," Langham said. "Now then, d'you notice anything else different about her?"

Oliver flashed his beam over the woman once more. It pissed him off that he didn't know her name yet, but that would come in time – *if* she decided to contact him again.

Oh, God. Her boots had been removed.

"Um, yes. Shit, yes. When I was last here, she had boots on. Hiking boots. One was tied tight, the other untied." Dread pooled in his stomach. "I interrupted the killer, didn't I? When I arrived..." He glanced at Langham.

He nodded. "Seems that way. And that's something that hasn't happened before. You felt different lately? Like your ability is evolving?"

He shook his head. "No, I feel the same. She called me like the others did. Woke me, said... Oh, Jesus."

"What?"

"She said she was *being* killed, not that she was dead. I didn't... I just didn't think anything of it. I got up as usual and came out here after she told me where to go. Then nothing." He swallowed. "So I got here and waited for her to speak to me again, and she did. Well, she never said anything, just laughed at something I said or thought, can't remember now, and then... Then she realised she was dead and she hasn't spoken since."

"Okay." Langham lifted a hand and rested it on Oliver's

shoulder. "Right. How long did it take you to get here?"

"I don't know. Ten minutes? Maybe twenty? Shitty traffic diversions." And all that time, while Oliver had travelled without any rush, this woman had been fighting for her life. "Damn. Just... Fuck it!"

"You weren't to know. This is a first for you."

Oliver eyed the corpse, eyes glazing. "So I disturbed the killer, and what? He ran off? Waited in the fucking bushes while I stood here? Went off and got his bloody car to waste some time until I'd finished? He took a risk, didn't he? I could have called you right away, right here. Jesus!" He slapped an open palm to his thigh and turned away, shirking off Langham's touch and looking out onto the road. "Your buddies are here, Detective."

"Is there anything else different, Oliver?"

Reluctantly, he slowly spun around. "Yes. Her legs are straight. They were at odd angles before. Her arms too." He studied her some more. "And fuck me, but her stomach wasn't anything like that."

"Like what?"

"Split open and bleeding. It was a normal stomach. I remember thinking she must have liked the gym because it was so toned."

"Right. And that's all?"

Oliver panned the flashlight beam farther up. *Oh, Jesus Christ...* "No, that's *not* all. Last time she had a face."

What the hell had he stumbled on this time? It had been bad enough seeing the woman as she had been, let alone how she was now. Oh, Oliver had seen sights like this one plenty of times, but not just after they'd been carried out. Not when they'd been done to the body while he'd sat in his fucking car several feet away, thinking of where to put the information in his mind so he could cope with what he'd seen. And now he'd have to do that all over again, compartmentalise, except he'd have a whole heap of guilt to go along with it. Why hadn't he sensed something was wrong? Why hadn't the woman contacted him to say what was happening?

Why—a cruel word that sometimes had no answers.

He faced the road again and watched several officers navigate their way across the grass. One, a detective in his usual impeccable suit, bugged the shit out of him, and he closed his eyes momentarily to quell the irritation he always made him feel. He was an arrogant son of a bitch who tolerated Oliver, was one of the many who had scoffed at his ability in the beginning. The one who was still a thorn in his side and made no bones about the fact that he thought Oliver had been involved in all the murders so far. Just that he couldn't prove it. What an arsehole.

He stopped in front of Oliver, eyes narrowed, the look on his face telling him he suspected him yet again.

"Ah, so it's one of *yours*, is it?" he said, lacing his hands in front of him and rocking on the balls of his feet.

Shields would be pissed off when he saw the amount of mud up the sides of his shoes and on the hems of his trousers. Oliver smiled at the possibility of seeing Shields' reaction to that.

"Might have known when Langham called it in," Shields continued.

"Whatever, Shields. You think what you like. This has nothing to do with me." Oliver presented his back to him, knowing it would piss the bastard off.

"So," Shields said, moving to stand between Oliver and Langham. "What do we have here?"

Langham cleared his throat. "Oliver was called out and—"

Shields chuckled. "Called out. I just love the way you use that term."

"Oliver was called out and it seems he disturbed the killer this time."

"Is that right?" Shields asked, jabbing Oliver in the ribs.

"Yes."

"So it isn't that someone disturbed *you?*" Shields tilted his head and stared at Oliver, a little too hard for his liking.

"No, I wasn't disturbed. I came out, as usual, saw her here and went back to my car to call it in."

He related what had followed, ignoring Shields' look of disbelief and the sneer on his fleshy lips. His dark, slicked-back hair was rigid, like he'd doused it with a can of hairspray prior to coming out, and he stank of freshly applied cologne. The cheap kind that cost a couple of quid on the market.

Oliver held back a snort of derision. "And then we came back and found her like this."

"Right. I see." Shields hunkered down, hands draped between his open knees. "So, let's go with what you've said. Let's say you're telling the truth. Now ask this poor bitch who did it and save us a lot of hassle."

Oliver sighed and flared his nostrils. "You know it doesn't work like that."

"Convenient," Shields said. "Gives your accomplices time to get away. I mean, think about it." He rose and towered above him. "These dead people never seem to speak to you again until a couple days after they've been killed. Now why is that?"

"I don't know. Maybe they need time to adjust. Maybe they have to pass over to wherever the fuck they go to when they die. I don't know. And I don't appreciate your tone."

"I don't care what you appreciate, Mr Armand. I don't care about anything but nailing you."

"That's enough!" Langham stepped between them. "You know damn well Oliver isn't involved in this shit, and it isn't something you should be discussing out here anyway. We have work to do, a scene to secure, evidence to find before it pisses down with rain. Arguing just halts the process. Let Oliver do his thing and you do yours."

"Testy," Shields said, squatting at the victim's feet again. "So what did she look like before she had her face sliced off?"

"Pretty. Like a doll." Oliver bit his lip, damned if he'd let himself buckle in front of Shields.

"You can give a description?" Shields rounded his shoulders.

"Of course I damn well can!"

"Christ, you're testy too. What's up with the pair of you?"

"You!" Oliver snapped, stalking away so he could be alone.

At the road, he leaned against Langham's car. God, if he killed anyone it would be Shields. A giggle echoed inside his head.

Thank fuck!

"Hey you," Oliver said. "How're you doing?"

No response.

"Can I at least have a name? Yours? His?"

"I don't know him."

"Oh, right. Any clue as to why he chose you?"

"Something to do with work."

"Which is?"

"PrivoLabs."

"Ah. You a scientist?"

"No. A secretary."

"And he works there?"

"No."

"But he knows someone who does?"

"Maybe."

"Love, you need to be a bit more specific."

"Yes, he must do. I…I knew something."

"And…?"

"He shut me up."

"What did you know?"

"I can't tell you. He said if I told you –"

"Hey, I don't want to rub it in here, but you're dead. He can't hurt you anymore, so if you tell me –"

"No, he knows about you. He said he'd looked you up in his car. Your number plate. His laptop. If I tell you anything, he'll hurt my son."

"Wait a minute. He knows about me?"

"Yes, he said if I thought about telling the psychic faggot after

26

I'm gone, he'd know. I can't… I made you find me, that was enough. And he knows. He came back after you went to your car."

"I noticed."

"He told me then if I told you anything else…"

"I see."

"I have to go."

"No, wait! Just wait a damn minute. What's with the sugar strands?"

"I can't tell you. I'm sorry, but I just can't. My son…"

"Shit!" Oliver made his way back to the scene. Once there, he caught Langham's attention and told him the latest news.

"So we have something, at least." Langham pinched his chin between finger and thumb. "PrivoLabs. You fancy coming along with me?"

"Yeah. After I've showered and got rid of these shoes."

"Ah, yes, the shoe thing. Okay. Let's go."

Chapter Three

The sun had brightened the sky and chased away the darkness of the last few hours, but it hadn't erased them from Oliver's mind. No, they'd remain there until this case was over, until he could file them in a mind box labelled 'FORGET', although that never really worked. Still, he tried to put solved cases to the back of his mind, told himself the dead were at peace once he'd helped them, and that was all he could do. A person could only help so much. After all the Ts were crossed and the Is dotted, the victims either had to find their own way or linger. He couldn't force them to move on, could only block them out to make way for new ones. And shit, he wished there were never any new ones. Wished no one had to die the way they did.

Dressed in clean clothing and freshly showered, he stared up at the PrivoLabs building, Langham beside him. The sun bounced off the blue-tinted windows, of which there were too many to count. The structure stretched into the sky like an accusing finger, the roof obscured by puffy clouds that spoke of snow on the way. Fucking brilliant. With no car, he'd be forced to walk everywhere, and he didn't own a pair of boots suitable for such weather. He'd have to buy some when he went to shop for some new Nikes. Or borrow Langham's car. He had access to one from the police pool, so it wasn't like he'd be reduced to working on foot.

"You ready?" Langham asked, walking up the grey marble steps to the double-wide glass front doors.

"As I'll ever be."

Langham pushed one door open and held it so Oliver could step inside. Allowing it to close behind them, he muttered, "As usual, keep your mouth shut, your eyes open and your mind tuned for the victim to contact you."

"Her name was Louise, not 'the victim'."

Shields had done his job and secured an ID, informing them of her identity as they'd driven through the city towards PrivoLabs. He'd also made sure Louise's son was in a secure place under protection, with Louise's mother. At least the arsehole had done something that didn't bug Oliver.

As they approached the reception desk, Langham gently cleared his throat. He leaned on the polished wood and asked to see the manager, flashing his badge to a startled receptionist, who nodded and lifted the phone handset to her ear. Oliver left him to it, idly glancing around to get a feel for the place. The glass walls appeared clear, nothing like the blue they were outside. Leather sofas dotted the area, black and plush, and if Oliver wasn't here for any reason but to crash out, he'd climb on one of them and sleep the sleep of the dead. He mentally cursed himself for his turn of phrase and eyed the many potted plants, tall ferns and coconut palms, the leaves lush enough to hide a person. This outfit raked in the money, that was for sure.

"Uh, Oliver?"

He turned at the sound of Langham's voice and smiled as he walked towards him. "Are we off to do some questioning, then?"

"Um, we would be if Louise had worked here and we had any tangible evidence something was amiss here."

"What?"

"She never worked here, Oliver."

"But she said—"

"I know what she said, but there isn't any record of her ever being here. Are you sure she said she actually worked *here*?"

Oliver thought back. Crap. "Well, no. She said she was killed because of something to do with work, then mentioned PrivoLabs. Shit. Sorry." Something had been way off ever since Louise had woken him with the call. His lack of concentration. Missing crucial information, like whether cars were parked on the side of the damn road. And now there was another misdemeanour to add to his growing list. He'd misinterpreted what Louise had said, bringing them out on a trip they needn't have made.

To make himself feel better, he said, "Can't we question the manager anyway?" When Langham didn't answer, he went on with, "Well, didn't you check my information first? Didn't Shields run her name through the database and confirm where she worked?"

"No. Your information is usually correct so we didn't—"

"Ah. Right. My fault. My fuck-up is going to go down *so* well with Shields. He'll gloat like the bastard he is."

"Fuck Shields."

"No thanks."

Oliver stormed out of the building, angry with himself and feeling as though he was losing his touch. It wouldn't be so bad if he didn't have to deal with this kind of thing—the voices, the messages—but if he were losing his grip, it would have to wait until he'd helped solve this case. Maybe he just needed sleep. A solid few hours where he wasn't interrupted.

Langham came up behind him and laid a hand on his back. The heat from his touch comforted Oliver, and he wanted nothing more than to bury his face in the crook of Langham's neck and have all this go away. He'd hugged Oliver in the past, all muscled arms and firm chest, and it had felt like nothing else existed except them. He'd entertained the idea of telling him how he felt about him, but it would only complicate things. What if Langham didn't feel the same? There would be tension between them, totally different to the sexual kind that simmered now, and Oliver couldn't handle ruining what they had, working by his side knowing Langham was aware he thought about him in *that* way.

"Listen, don't beat yourself up," Langham said. "Shit

happens."

"Yeah, it usually does to me, but not like this."

"Anything on your mind?" He steered Oliver towards his car and opened the passenger door, ushering him inside.

Oliver stared up at him from the seat. "That's a stupid question, Langham. One of the worst you've come out with. There's *always* something on my mind."

He smiled. "Not like that. Not the voices. I mean worries. Shit you need to talk about."

"What, like me fucking up? No, I don't want to talk about that." He stared out of the windshield, jaw rigid and hands bunched into fists in his lap. "You gonna stand there staring at me for much longer? I mean, it's cold out, and the door being open? You're letting in a draught."

Langham huffed out a breath. "You are one infuriating, irritating little—"

"Yeah, yeah. Get it all out. Purge your feelings. Let me know how you *really* feel, why don't you." Oliver knew he was pushing him, but he could never help himself. It was fun, something they just *did* to one another, and when the car door slammed and Langham strode around the front of the car, Oliver let out his tension in a burst of laughter.

Langham climbed inside the car then started the engine. "Glad you find it funny."

"Of course I do. So would you if the boot was on the other foot."

"Bitch."

"Bastard."

Langham peeled away from the kerb, chuckling himself. "You're too hard on yourself, you know that?"

"Yep."

"Don't you think you ought to loosen up?"

"Why, do you?"

"Maybe."

"Oh, right. So not only am I infuriating and irritating, I'm a tight-arse. Great if some guy winds up with me and likes a tight hole, but... You know what, you have the most

31

charming way of saying things."

"As do you."

"So, what next?"

"We go back to the station and find out where the victim—"

"Louise."

"The *victim* worked. Then we go from there."

"Why don't you ever call them by their names?" Oliver looked across at him, noting his firm jaw, the way a muscle flicked beneath his skin.

"Because then it becomes personal. I don't do personal."

"Ain't that the truth," Oliver muttered.

Langham glanced at him then returned his attention to the road. "You got something you need to say?"

"Nope."

"Oh, right. I could have sworn you did."

"Nope."

Langham smiled and drew to a stop at a red light. "Listen, you know I care about you, don't you?"

He'd never said it outright before, and Oliver took a few seconds to digest what he'd said. He could mean anything— that he cared for him as a friend, a colleague. "Yes."

"And friends confide in one another, don't they?"

"Yes."

"So if you ever need to confide—"

"Yep, I know."

"Good, just so you do."

They spent the remainder of the journey in silence, Oliver fighting the urge to have a tantrum. It was insane, wasn't it? To have a fit because Langham thought of him as just a friend? Just because Oliver wanted more, because he'd stupidly allowed himself to grow attached to him in the last six months, it didn't mean... Didn't mean shit.

As soon as the car drew to a stop, Oliver hauled arse, striding towards the station with purpose. He'd help solve this case then inspect his feelings later. This wasn't the time to get all worked up over something he couldn't change.

He had a job to do, and as soon as Louise contacted him again, they'd need to be ready. He shoved the door open then made his way towards Langham's office, knowing the detective wouldn't be far behind. There, he slumped into Langham's chair and plonked his feet on the desk, crossing his legs at the ankles. His head itched, and he snatched off his hat, tossing it across the room and watching it fall to the floor.

Langham walked in and eyed him from the doorway. "Why do you always insist on doing that?"

"Doing what?" he asked, pretending to pick at a hangnail.

"Sitting in my chair with your feet on my desk. Look, you're scrunching my papers."

"Oh, really? I hadn't noticed. Sorry about that."

Oliver planted his feet on the floor and scooted the chair across the room, picking up his hat so he had something to occupy his hands. Langham was suddenly too close. Being in the room with him, his presence overwhelming, his scent doing things to Oliver it shouldn't be doing. Like making him wish he was in his arms, breathing it in with his head resting on Langham's shoulder.

"He's sweet, I'll give you that."

Oliver sat upright, startled that Louise had decided to contact him now. "Hey, Louise. You all right?" He noted Langham's raised eyebrows and put a finger to his lips so he'd remain quiet.

"I'm okay."

"So, we went to PrivoLabs and found out you didn't work there. You want to tell me where you did work?" Oliver closed his eyes, bouncing his heels on the floor and hoping for a positive answer.

"He said – "

"I know, love, but it doesn't matter what you tell me now. Your son is safe."

"He is?"

"Yes. He's living with your mother."

"My mother? Oh no…not her…"

33

"What's up with that? You two not get along? She's all your son has now, he has nowhere else to go. We've moved them both to a secure location. He won't find them."

"Oh, God."

"That's all right. You're welcome." He couldn't help his sarcasm.

"He'll know she has him."

"It's okay. Don't worry about that. He won't find them. So, do you think you can tell me what you know?"

"I'd been filing and a piece of paper fell out. I shouldn't have looked, should have just put it back inside the file, but I held about three and wasn't sure which one it came from. So I read it and saw…"

Oliver waited a few beats. Louise didn't continue, so he prompted, "Saw…?"

"They're doing experiments."

"Who are?"

"PrivoLabs."

"Yep, that's what they do, right?"

"Yes, but these ones… What I read were notes. They probably weren't even meant to be in the file. Handwritten. Doodles."

"So what are they doing? What tests are they?"

"They're drugging children. Older youths."

Oliver jumped up from the chair and began to pace. Langham grabbed a notebook and pen from his desk and held them out to him, but he waved them away. "With what?" His heart pattered fast and he felt sick to his stomach.

"With this stuff. Like… God, you're not going to believe me. She didn't…"

"Try me."

"With this stuff to make them do things."

"Do things?"

"Yes. Bad things. They want to see whether the drugs make the children kill. I never thought… I never suspected…"

"What?" Oliver stilled, bile in his throat and a sour feeling in his gut. This kind of shit didn't happen, did it? Not for real.

34

"He's taken the drugs too. The man who…"

"Shit. You got a name?"

"I don't know his name."

"What about the name of the person who wrote the notes."

"There wasn't one."

"So how did anyone find out what you knew?"

"I gave the note to my boss."

"And what happened then?"

"He started an investigation. Got PrivoLabs' attention with it. He got fired."

"What's his name?"

"Mr Reynolds. Mark Reynolds."

"Right, thank you. Anything else you can remember?"

"He…ah, he came to my house."

"Who, Reynolds?"

"No, the man. The man who…"

"Right."

"He told me I had to go with him, leave my son asleep. And he said if I didn't, he'd give my son that stuff. The sugar strands."

"Oh, Jesus. Okay. Do you want to talk about what he did to you?"

"Not really."

"But can you at least tell me something about him so we can catch this son of a bitch?"

"He was tall. Very tall. Big hands. He smelt…"

"What of?"

"Musty clothing. Like he lived in a dirty place."

"What did he look like?"

"I don't know. He wore a mask and a wig."

So it *was* that fucker who had tried to run Oliver off the road. If he'd been given shit to make him kill, it explained why he'd been intent on crashing into Oliver's car. Why he'd killed Louise — although he'd clearly had another reason for getting rid of her. Louise had been in the wrong place at the wrong time, discovering something she shouldn't have — and look where it had got her. It made Oliver wonder about the virtues of being honest and doing the right thing.

Sometimes it was best to just keep your goddamn mouth shut.

"*I wish I had.*"

"Sorry, Louise. I didn't mean for you to hear that."

"*It's okay.*"

"No, it's not."

"*I'm tired. This is hard work.*"

"I know, love. Can you try for one last bit of information for me? Something about him that stands out? Louise? Louise, are you there?" Oliver stood still, straining to hear a response, a whisper, anything. Silence. "Fuck it!"

"Has she gone?" Langham moved as though to walk towards him then changed his mind.

"Yes. Damn it, yes!" Oliver flopped back into the chair, rage bubbling inside him over thoughts of the hateful things people did to others. Killing. Hurting. What the hell was *wrong* with people? Why did they feel the need to *do* shit like that?

"So, when you're ready…" Langham took a folding chair from against the wall and set it up behind his desk. He rested his elbows on his blotter, steepled his long fingers and propped his chin on the tips.

"Give me a second." Oliver jammed his fingers in his hair. "I need to remember everything she said. I don't need another fuck-up on my résumé."

Langham failed at stifling a sigh.

"You got a problem with that?" Oliver snapped.

"No, but it seems you do."

"You're damn right I do. I don't *do* wrong, okay? I don't *do* fucking up."

"I know, and you don't usually, so cut yourself a damn break, will you? Concentrate on what she told you, tell me, then we can get the ball rolling."

He decided to ignore the 'usually' comment. Getting into a fight with Langham wouldn't solve this case, although it would give Oliver an outlet to vent his frustration. But no, he wasn't going there.

Not yet anyway.

Chapter Four

Langham stared at Oliver, one eyebrow raised, and took his elbows off the desk. "So, we're talking some freaky shit here, right? If the victim's meant to be believed, this guy took something that *made* him kill?" He sighed then stood, gazing at some spot or other on the carpet, pinching his chin.

"Something more interesting in the damn carpet pile?" Oliver asked, frustrated and angrier than he'd been in a long while.

Louise had given just enough information to make him want to catch this fucker quickly, catch the people doing those experiments. Using sugar strands was ingenious. Lacing food with them, food kids liked to eat. Where were they distributing these doughnuts or whatever the fuck they put the strands on? A shop? Free on some stall? In PrivoLabs itself?

Langham's apparent lack of concern, his almost languid perusal of worn-down carpet fibres and his clearly obvious incredulousness over the drug thing pissed Oliver the hell off.

"I mean," Oliver said, "there's only Louise to consider here. Only a dead woman who died because she knew something she shouldn't. Only a kid left without a mother — a kid currently in hiding with his grandmother, who has to put aside her grieving to make sure she does everything right for the kid. Only a load of other kids and their parents suffering at the hands of some mental bastards. Hey, staring at the carpet is a great solution. Yeah, it really helps solve the case." He stood abruptly and paced. "You're getting on my fucking nerves staring at the floor like that."

Langham gave Oliver a dark look—one of the darkest he'd ever been given. "I'll ignore that outburst. Put it down to you being tired and overprotective of the victim. Distraught over the kids being plied with drugs. Looking at the carpet, staring into space helps me—"

"Overprotective? Over-fucking-protective? Are you deliberately trying to rile me?" Oliver moved to the door and curled his hand around the knob, his intent to storm out. Langham wouldn't solve this case as fast without him, and Oliver had a mind to follow the leads himself. Anything to get something done and done now.

Langham strode up behind him, covering Oliver's hand with his. "Listen, you're flying high on adrenaline, with the need to get to the bottom of this *now*, but you *know* it doesn't work like that. You get like this every time, and every time I tell you the same thing. Slow down. Think things through. And we'll get there. We always do."

Langham's voice, the timbre and reverberation of sound, went straight to Oliver's cock. Angry that the detective's closeness, his words, had switched him from pissed off to horny in a heartbeat, Oliver silently berated himself. Louise was dead, had come to him for help, and here he was getting a hard cock instead.

He sighed, blew out hard and long. *Get a fucking grip. Life goes on after someone dies. Cocks don't stay soft just because… shit, they just don't stay soft.*

"You're right," he said. "As usual. And I *hate* admitting that, you know that, don't you?"

Langham's chuckle should have incensed Oliver more, should have made him yank the door open and strut out never to return, but it didn't. No, he remained where he was, soaking up the remnants of that laugh as it lingered in his mind, all around him. In his groin.

"Shit! Langham, you fuck me the hell off, you know that?"

"Yep."

Langham drew closer, his breath warming Oliver's neck.

Damn it, but Oliver was lost now. Lost in Langham's closeness. His scent, that spicy, tangy aroma that was a mix of cologne and fresh sweat. The heat of the detective's hand as it tightened over his. The press of an erection to his backside.

Jesus Christ… For the love of God…

"You need to, uh, step away, Langham."

"I do?"

There it was again, that tone of voice, hardening Oliver's cock some more.

"Yeah. Step the hell away before we—"

"Do something we'll regret?"

"Something like that."

"So you'd regret it, is that what you're saying?"

"Yes. No. I mean… Crap! Of course I wouldn't bloody regret it. But you might."

"What makes you think that?"

If Langham didn't take a step back and remove that hard-on from Oliver's arse… Now wasn't the time, was it? To indulge in a fuck, or at the very least some frantic petting. Oliver's mind went into overdrive. This was the first time Langham had crossed the invisible line between them, one that had always been there without them ever having to mention it. Yeah, they'd flirted, made it clear they liked one another, but shit, why was Langham acting like this today? Why now? What had made him step up to the plate when he'd said he cared for him as a *friend?*

Oliver's heart raced at the same speed as the questions firing through his mind. "Um, you've never…never come this close to me before. Not like this. Not—"

"With my cock hard? That what you were going to say?"

"Well, no, but you have a point."

"Hell, yeah, I have a damn point, and it's throbbing like a son of a bitch."

Oliver imagined that point, that rounded tip of a cock he'd only ever dreamt about. Yeah, he'd studied the swell of it as it rested beneath Langham's zipper—studied it on more than one occasion when the detective's attention had been on anything but Oliver's face — but this? Imagining it like this? When it was so close?

Fuck.

He turned, removing his hand from the doorknob and instantly regretting the loss of skin contact. Still, pressed chest to chest with Langham instead wasn't something to be sniffed at. Having Langham look at him, staring deep into his eyes the way he was... That more than made up for skin on skin. Oliver knew the signs of lust when he saw them, just not on Langham's face, and it was alien seeing them there. Oh, he'd imagined that, too, the look he was getting now, but had never thought he'd receive it. They worked together, had a drink in a bar after a long day's work, got close to one another in the car, arms brushing as Langham shifted gears, but nothing like this.

Nothing so sexual and goddamn erotic.

"It's about time we acknowledged this," Langham said, lifting his hands to cup them on Oliver's shoulders.

He needs to take those hands away. If he doesn't... "It is? Oh, right."

What else could he say? He hadn't been expecting this. If he had, maybe he could have come out with one of his witty answers, some retort to have Langham laughing, have them back on the even keel they had been on before. Instead, he was floundering for something to say that wouldn't offend Langham, but at the same time would get the detective to walk away. Although, maybe that wasn't such a good idea. His cock pressed against Oliver's was damn fine, and he wondered what it would feel like without clothing between them.

Hot. Soft.

And he wanted it.

"There's something there, Oliver, between us."

"There's something between us all right," he said, trying for lightness, a little banter to ease the raging ache inside him. "But now isn't, uh, the time to—"

"Do anything about it?"

"Yeah."

"You're right, of course, but it doesn't stop me wanting to get my cock out, get yours out, and—"

"Okay, enough!" Oliver put his hands on Langham's chest—fuck, that felt good—and gently pushed him away. He cursed himself immediately, but shit, anyone could knock on the door at any time. "Someone might catch us doing something we shouldn't." He strode away to his chair, hoping that Louise would come back so he could concentrate on her instead of his engorged dick and the feelings swimming through him.

"Shouldn't?" Langham followed him, planted his hands on the armrests and loomed over Oliver. "That what you think? That we shouldn't?"

Oliver looked up at him, lost again in those damn eyes. "Not shouldn't. I meant… You *know* what I meant. We're working. We need to concentrate on that, not—"

"Having a hard and hot fuck."

Oliver's stomach rolled over. Man, Langham's one sentence had him undecided on what the hell to do. This was an opportunity to put an end to the sexual tension between them, to assuage the gnawing, sexy-as-fuck beat inside him, to stop their delicate dance and make whatever they felt official. Out in the open.

"Yeah. Here isn't the right place. If we get caught you'd be raked over the bloody coals. Lose your job for fucking in your office. Not a good move, man."

Langham straightened, took his hands off the chair arms. "Put like that, I can see your point."

He stared at the carpet again, only this time it didn't piss Oliver off. He was glad of the space between them. The silence.

Langham looked up, straight at Oliver. "So if I walk away now, will it be another six months of knowing you before we get that close again? You going to dilly-dally about, avoiding the issue?"

"No. If we're in a different place and something happens, then yeah, I can deal with that." *I think.*

"So we're done just for now."

"Yeah. Just for now."

"Good."

In less time than it took Oliver to swallow the lump of emotion in his throat, Langham was all business again. He walked over to his desk and sat, hands splayed on his blotter.

"So, as we were discussing before… Someone's feeding people drugs that make them kill. The first, as far as we know, is someone who wears a wig and mask."

"It isn't all that inconceivable, the drug thing," Oliver said, leaning forward to hide his erection that didn't fancy going away any time soon. "I mean, look at me. Look what I do. There's no explanation for that. Might not be a reason why drugs can turn people into killers."

"Yeah, but speaking to the dead… Lots of people have that ability. Lots of people have been able to prove the dead exist by what they get told. But a man going around dressed as a fucking woman, made to kill by some chemical? No, I don't believe that shit."

"Many things seem unbelievable. Take this, for instance. Demons and shit exist. I know — I've spoken to one."

"You have?"

"Yeah, years ago, but it wasn't a pleasant experience. And I saw him in my head. He showed himself to me. His eyes glowed."

Langham huffed out a laugh — of hilarity or nervousness, Oliver wasn't sure.

"Okay." Langham stood and paced in front of Oliver. "We can talk about that another time, if you like. So what now?"

"How do I fucking know? I need Louise to come back, tell me more."

"And that might be in the next few minutes, an hour, three days or not at all. We can't rely on her. Got to do something ourselves."

"I know that, and I wanted to before you... Look, forget the ins and outs of why the drugs work. They just do. We've got other information to go on. PrivoLabs doing experiments on kids. They're somehow getting children to eat food with sugar strands on them — they've got to contain the drugs. Sick much?"

"Yeah, but that's a bit delicate, going to Privo. We can't just storm in there and demand they show us their experiment records."

"Why not?"

"We don't have proof they're doing anything, so we can't get a warrant. Use your damn head, Oliver. All we have is some dead woman's word."

Langham had a point — another, less visible one — but Oliver believed Louise, knew she was telling the truth.

"We do have proof. That guy left those strands on Louise's body."

"Fuck, yeah." Langham snatched up the phone and barked orders to some unfortunate on the other end. He slammed the phone down. "Forensics will be on it...when they're on it. No sense of bloody haste, that lot."

"So, while we wait, we interview Mark Reynolds. Then Louise's kid — he might have seen the guy when he went to her house. Jeez, who's the fucking detective here, me or you?"

Langham shot him another dark look. "I'll ignore that comment too. Put it down to sexual frustration."

Oliver opened his mouth to give the detective what for, then closed it again as Langham's laugh filled the room.

"Fuck you, Langham."

"Yeah, you will do." He smiled. "In the meantime, we have someone to ask a shitload of questions."

"Mark Reynolds?"

"Damn fucking right it's Mark Reynolds."

Chapter Five

Funny how they went straight back into work mode. Out of the office and in Langham's car, Oliver was less horny and more focused. Unease at interviewing a guy who might not want to answer their questions made him shift a little in his seat. What if the bloke had been threatened to keep quiet? What if Langham had to haul his arse into the police station in order to get some answers? Even then the man might not play ball. Fright would keep his mouth shut. Shit, if some guy with murder in his eyes had told Oliver to zip it, he'd damn well zip it.

Langham drove out of the city, their journey taking them to some out-of-the-way place called Lower Repton Oliver had only heard of but not visited. A tiny hamlet wasn't his ideal destination, but he was pleasantly surprised by the quaintness of the area. Cottages flanked the roadside, and a small, Cotswold stone pub, Pickett's Inn, sat hunched on the bend in the road like a decrepit old man, its roof bowed, walls bulging outward.

Oliver shuddered. The place might be quaint, but something was off here. He sensed many spirits lurking nearby and imagined there *would* be a fair few, what with the hamlet being so old. People would have lived here all their lives, dying in their beds.

"Um, which cottage is his?" he asked, anxious to get this interview over and done with. The vibes he was getting freaked him the hell out. "I don't like it here."

"Me neither. Maybe it's the remoteness, but I wouldn't live here if you paid me." As they slowly drove along, Langham leant forward over the steering wheel and peered at the cottages. "None of them are numbered. Just named. Reynolds' records said he lived at number two, but it's anyone's guess which end of the road number two is."

"You could get out and ask." Oliver nodded at an elderly woman in her front garden, who had come out to nose at what they were doing, no doubt. She held a watering can, which she'd tipped as though she'd really come out to wet the plants, except no water drizzled from the spout. "She'll know which one we're looking for."

Langham drew up to the roadside outside the woman's aged wooden picket fence and wound down his window. "Excuse me, madam. Which house is number two?"

She squinted and ground her unquestionably false teeth, wispy strands of hair escaping her bun. Her lips looked elasticated, undulating like that. "What you want to know for? Who are you?"

"I'm Detective Langham," he said, whipping out his badge and showing her. "And I need to speak to the resident. Mark Reynolds?"

"Ain't seen him. Not since the last copper came along to speak to him, and *he* looked familiar. Like I'd seen him before somewhere."

Oliver's stomach clenched, and his arsehole bunched as a wave of nausea came over him. "Something's fucking off. I feel it."

"You and me both, man," Langham said out of the side of his mouth, then to the woman, "Another policeman was here?"

"Yes, I just said so, didn't I?" She tsked and rolled her eyes. "No idea how you people solve crimes if you can't even process a simple sentence. Yes, another policeman. Badge just like yours. And Mark lives back there. Second house in on the other side of the road." She marched down her path towards her house, turning to stare at them when she reached her front door.

"Thank the Lord for nosey old bitches, but fuck me, she's mean as hell," Langham muttered.

"Yeah, well, mean or not, let's interview this bloke and get out of here. This place…it isn't nice. There are too many ghosts here. I can feel them all trying to speak to me."

Langham made a U-turn in the deserted road. "So let them in. Maybe we'll learn something."

Oliver widened his eyes. "Are you fucking serious? You try having a few of them gossiping in your head all at once. Fuck you."

"Fuck you too, you moody wanker." Langham smiled, parking outside number two, the wooden plaque beside the front door announcing the cottage as Reynolds' Gaff.

The feeling of wrongness was stronger here. This wasn't unusual in itself. Many places he visited when questioning people with Langham felt this way—just not as strong. Or sinister.

"This is one nasty-arsed case," he mumbled.

"And the others we've worked on weren't?" Langham cut the engine and slipped off his seatbelt.

"They were, but this one… I don't know. It's hard to explain."

"Then don't. Soak it all up, see what you get when we go in, and tell me once we've left. I'll do the talking. You just concentrate on picking shit up."

Langham got out of the car, and Oliver did the same, his stomach heavy with dread. He hated this part of investigations. Negative energy always found him, and he saw sights and heard sounds no one should. Terrible things, horrible noises. Voices.

After walking up the paved path bordered by a well-kept garden with a recently mown lawn and pruned hedges, the pair stood on a shiny, red-brick step.

Langham glanced at Oliver before knocking. "Got anything yet?"

"At the risk of sounding cheesy, just the feeling of impending doom, only more so. You know, the usual. Something being majorly off, knowing we're going to find out some shit we hadn't expected."

"Right." Langham knocked again. "Good."

They waited a minute.

"Wonder if he's out?" Langham walked across to the large window beside the door, presumably the living room. "Whoa. If he's out, he needs to tidy up when he gets home. Looks like someone's had an unfriendly visit."

"Shit." Oliver moved to stand beside him and stared through the glass. "Uh, yeah. Unfriendly is right. We going in?"

"Yep. Could be a man in distress inside, know what I mean?" He went back to the front door. Kicked the damn thing open as though the wood was nothing but flimsy cardboard.

Oliver almost, *almost* got hard again.

Pack it in! Focus on the job.

"I'll go first. Stay behind me," Langham said.

Oliver followed Langham inside, hit immediately by the stench of blood. He gagged, breathed through his mouth and stared around a small hallway littered with coats flung down from the hooks on the wall just inside the doorway. Someone had been here, that much was evident, and he didn't need the growing unease in his gut to tell him that. He stepped over the coats, tailing Langham into the living room. The mess here was worse—sofa overturned, the wall cabinet pulled down and balancing precariously on an armchair, contents strewn over a carpet covered in fluff from inside the throw cushions. One mental motherfucker had been in here looking for something, all right.

Langham turned, cocking his head to let Oliver know they'd find nothing here but chaos. Oliver followed him into the kitchen—more of the same wreckage there—then up the stairs. The detective coughed, gagged and stopped at the top, glancing across the landing at the two closed doors. Oliver stared at them through the baluster rails, a wave of hate flowing over him. The press of spirits wanting to speak to him made him breathless. He swallowed, knowing there was nothing to fear here with regards to another human being. No one was at home.

No living person, anyway.

"Someone's dead in there," he said as Langham turned to look down at him. "Probably Reynolds."

"Yeah, the smell's unmistakeable, but I told myself maybe he had a dog that had died or something. Ever the optimist, me."

Oliver smiled, holding back a rejoinder that would proclaim Langham anything *but* a bloody optimist. Now wasn't the time for their sniping. "Uh, he's in that room." He pointed to the door closest to Langham. A snapshot of what lay behind it flashed through his mind. "And it isn't pretty. You might want to take a few deep breaths. He's, um, he's a fucking mess." He swallowed down bile, shaking his head to remove the image, though why he bothered when he'd see it for real any second now he didn't know. Habit, he guessed.

"Right. Bloody wonderful." Langham walked towards the door, taking a tissue from his pocket to turn the handle. "Get ready to be hit in the face by the reek, man."

Oliver covered his nose and mouth. Langham opened the door, and, expecting the stench to override anything else, Oliver was shocked to find the smell was the last thing he needed to think about. Blood soaked the walls, near-black now it had dried, arcs and splashes, rivulets and streams that spoke of a violent death. The bed was soaked with it, the quilt looking hardened with the stuff, and the carpet was ebony in small, circular patches where the victim had possibly staggered around the room, falling every so often as his life had ebbed away.

But there was no corpse.

"What the fuck?" Oliver said, his frown hurting. "I saw him. Saw the man all cut up and shit. He was on the bed. Face up. Eyes open. Arms hacked off."

"Well, he isn't here now." Langham stepped back – right onto Oliver's toe.

"Shit! You might want to watch where you're stepping,

man."

"It would help if you wasn't right up my arse."

Oliver refused the bait. He was *not* going there with a ribald response. Not when they stood at the site of someone's death. And then it struck him. The press of spirits wasn't plural. It was one spirit. Reynolds. It had to be. "Uh, I'm going to let them in. Him in."

Langham spun to face him. "You got Reynolds on at you?"

"I think so."

"Then open the hell up! What are you waiting for?"

Oliver sighed and unlatched the locked door inside his mind. The spirit came tumbling in, as if he'd been leaning against it with all his might, and Oliver *felt* the spirit's disorientation as it fought to regain its equilibrium. Heavy breathing filled Oliver's mind, and the sense of a panicked man covered him in a heavy sweat.

"Calm down," he said. "Take a moment before you speak."

Oliver waited, staring at Langham. The detective's face showed how impatient he was for information, but this was Oliver's domain and he called the shots here. The breathing lightened, became less ragged, and a low humming began, like an abused kid trying to drown out the sound of his parents fighting.

"It's all right. Just take your time. We're not going anywhere. And we're here for you. To help catch who did this to you. I know it's difficult. Know how painful this is for you. How much hard work it is. But just focus on what you need to tell me, and if you can give me images, too, then that would be great. If not, no worries at all, okay?"

The humming stopped, leaving only the sound of breathing—from all three of them.

"Eyes like madness. Couldn't get over them, the way they flickered like that. Eyes like madness. Didn't used to be that way. Weird. Can't get to grips with it. Didn't like it. They weren't real. They were…freaky. He's been tested on, like those kids. He wasn't

like he was before…he said…he…"

"It's okay. Slow down. Just take a deep breath and start at the beginning. Don't tell me about your death, either, tell me about him. Concentrate only on him."

This guy was going to burn out his connection if he wasn't careful, then Oliver and Langham would be left with fuck all new to go on. He quickly shielded his thoughts from Reynolds while he awaited his next outburst. It wouldn't do for the guy to feel under pressure.

A huge sigh filled Oliver's mind, then—

"Yes, he's been given that stuff I found out about. Been experimented on. He's like a super-human. Great strength. His eyes were okay until he…"

Another sigh.

"Mustn't think about the death, only him. Just think about him and what he's like. Yes… He had a woman's wig on. Some kind of mask or makeup. So he knows. Oh, yes, he knows he's doing wrong – otherwise, he wouldn't wear a disguise, right? He knows right from wrong, I know that. Yes, he was brought up right."

"You're doing well, Mark. Keep going."

Langham squeezed past Oliver and went to sit at the top of the stairs but changed his mind after staring down at the carpet. It was probably bloodied.

"I ripped his wig off when he… I ripped it off because he shouldn't be wearing that. Didn't suit him. Never wore one before. Pulled out some of his real hair. Saw that on TV once. They said if you were attacked to try and rip out some hair, scratch skin so it went under your nails, give the police something to go on. I did that. I was right, wasn't I? Right to do that? Even though it was him… Maybe I shouldn't have tried ratting him out like that."

"Yes, Mark. Excellent. You did good. So where are you?"

"I'm here with you."

"No, where is your body?"

"He took me out of here. Put me in a van."

"Think about the van. What colour is it?"

"Um, yeah, think. It was red. Dark red. Small van, like a car without back seats. You know the kind I mean? He's had it a

while. Remember when he showed it to me before…"

"Go on."

"He took me to this field. Muttered something about some bitch being dumped up the way a bit. I didn't know who he meant, but I'm guessing I wasn't his first. Didn't think he'd come for me. Not him. Thought he was someone else — never thought he'd be like that."

"Who? It's like you know him."

Silence.

"Was there a river nearby, Mark?"

"Yes. I'm… My body's on a bend of the river. It's… I'm half in the water, half out. Like, my hands are in the water."

"Fuck."

"What? What did I say wrong?"

"Nothing. It's fine. Keep going." Oliver thought of the water doing its damage, possibly taking away those hairs, that skin beneath Mark's nails. The killer knew exactly what Mark had been up to.

"He said, 'There. A little bit of sweetness for you.' Then he sprinkled some of those things on me. You know the kind I mean?"

"No. What things."

"Those things you get on cakes. Sprinkles over icing."

"Sugar strands?"

"Yes, that's it. He said Grandmother used to pour them into his mouth when he'd been bad. Said they filled his mouth so he had trouble breathing. And she wouldn't let him spit them out. He had to sit there until they melted. He said he wouldn't make me eat them, just sprinkled them on me so everyone would know I'd been bad. But he's lying. She never did that. And he told me it was ironic the medication was in the same form. Like those strands were haunting him."

"How do you know he's lying? And you, bad? You didn't do anything wrong, Mark, except to try and make this right."

"I did. I poked into something I shouldn't have. Found out what they were doing. I'd been in his room before that woman at work showed me the notes. He'll come for you next because he knows

*you know. You and him over there. Be careful. He comes quietly –
he's right there before you even know it. With those eyes. And he
slices and cuts, stabs and chases you around until you can't get
away anymore. Until... Mustn't think about the death. Have to
concentrate only on him..."*

Mark's breathing intensified, alerting Oliver to his panic
returning.

"Well done, Mark. Now, think about that van. Did you
catch any of the licence plate? Anything about it that might
help us?"

"No. But I know where he lives. I know him."

"You do?" Jesus, why hadn't he fucking said so from the
start?

"Because I forgot."

"You weren't meant to hear that, Mark. I'm sorry."

"Right. You want to know where he lives, who he is?"

"We do." Oliver held his breath.

*"He lives in the basement of this old house. You know the one
I mean?"*

"No. Tell me."

*"It's in Saltwater Street. That old thing on the corner. The one
with the dirty windows with filthy net curtains. Grandmother
lives there."*

"Your grandmother?"

"Yes. She's still there. Old as the hills but there just the same."

"And his name?"

Mark sighed. *"Damn easy to answer that one. He's my
brother. Alex Reynolds."*

Chapter Six

Oliver staggered against the banister as Mark disappeared. The void his spirit left behind took a few moments to fill with questions, ones he knew Langham would also ask or ponder on out loud once he'd told him what Mark had said. Quickly, to save the detective battering him with queries, Oliver related the latest information.

"So," Oliver said when he'd finished, "do we have the same situation with Alex as we have with PrivoLabs? Only a dead man's word on Alex's guilt so we can't barge in and arrest him?"

"Something like that, but we *can* go and ask him if he knows where his brother is. Make it look like we're after Mark not Alex. The freaky-eyed fuck might slip up."

Oliver shivered. "Yeah, or he might well turn *into* that freaky-eyed fuck and do to us what he did to Louise and Mark. This guy sounds like he's been programmed to prevent people finding anything out about what Privo are up to. Except we've got a good idea—and really, we ought to think about telling Shields about this shit, just in case something happens to us and the information we have dies with us."

Langham stood and began his descent of the stairs. "Yeah, but if we tell him... You know what he's like. He'll poke his damn nose in, break the case and take all the credit."

"Rather that than us being dead, man," Oliver muttered, following him downstairs. Outside on the path, he asked, "You calling this in?"

Langham nosed about the garden, looking for God knew what. "Yep, so I guess Shields will hear about it anyway."

"Exactly. So call it in directly to him, save you repeating yourself, 'cause you know he'll want the ins and outs of the cat's arsehole if he hears the news from someone other than you. He can deal with this place while we head over to Alex's—and you *are* going to tell Shields where we're going, aren't you?"

"Yeah, yeah, quit your fucking nagging."

"Fuck you."

Oliver turned away with a smile, leaving Langham to call Shields. As the detective rattled off what they'd been up to and what they'd discovered, Oliver faced the cottage and closed his eyes. Maybe, if he concentrated, Mark would come back, or Louise. They'd given him excellent information, but he couldn't shake the feeling that this wasn't going to be a cut and dried case. Okay, Louise had given Mark the notes, and Mark had investigated, finding out a whole lot of info he hadn't expected. Louise had been killed over what she knew, Mark for the same reason, but how the hell did someone kill their own brother like that? Had Alex been changed so much by the experiments that he had lost the knowledge that Mark *was* his brother? Was he programmed to kill *anyone* who got in PrivoLabs' way? Oliver thought so, but he also knew Alex must have been one fucked-up motherfucker before Privo had got hold of him. If the tale about the grandmother and those sugar strands were true, that man had serious issues he needed to deal with. They were spilling over into his kills, which meant the experiments hadn't succeeded in taking away every part of him, the basic essence of who he'd been before.

So, what was the point in PrivoLabs' experiment? To allow people to seem relatively normal until someone needed killing? To have them act as they would prior to the experiments, and some switch or whatever was flicked, turning the human lab rats into freaks who went about doing abhorrent things? The owner of Privo was one sick bastard—if it was even him doing this shit—and Oliver couldn't wait to bring him down.

The snap of Langham's mobile phone closing brought Oliver out of his thoughts. He opened his eyes and turned to face the detective, who grimaced as though it had caused him pain to speak to Shields. Oliver knew that feeling. He hated the wanker with a vengeance.

"Come on, we've got to wait for someone to turn up here then we're going to Saltwater Street." Langham strode towards his car and got in.

Oliver stared for a moment in shock. Langham usually made some caustic remark about Shields when he'd spoken to him. Something had pissed him off for him to just walk away like that.

In the car, Oliver asked, "So, what's up?"

Langham started the engine, letting it idle while he stared ahead and flexed his jaw. Oliver watched the way the muscle flickered beneath the skin and fought the urge to lean over and lick it—lick up to that soft-as-fuck earlobe and suck it into his mouth. His cock twitched, and he brought the image of Mark dead on his bed to mind to stop his dick growing harder.

"You okay, man?" He kept his gaze on Langham.

"Will be in a minute. Just got to digest what that prick said."

Oliver remained silent, unwilling to press Langham. When he acted like this, it was best to leave him be—he'd come around in his own time. After several minutes sitting in silence, though, Oliver grew antsy for an answer. The distant wail of a police siren prevented him prompting Langham again, and he sat with his mouth firmly closed until the cops arrived to secure the scene.

Langham spoke to them through his window then sped off towards the city. Still silent. Oliver clamped his teeth shut. Bit his lip. Rubbed a spot on his jeans as though they were dirty.

He couldn't take this any longer. "Okay, so what did Shields say?"

"He knows I'm gay. That *we're* gay."

"What? How the fuck did *that* come up in conversation? What the shit has it got to do with this case?"

"Everything, according to him. Reckons we shouldn't be working together if we're fucking."

"But we're not!"

"No, but we will be."

Oliver stared ahead at the road speeding beneath them. "But he doesn't need to know that. We can keep it quiet. No bastard needs to know. We'll deny it. Simple. They can't prove anything unless they follow us around all damn day to see where we go and whether we stay over at one another's houses. Fuck, we haven't even *got* that far yet!" He sat quietly for a minute, then asked, "And like I just said, how did that come up in conversation?"

"I mentioned Alex Reynolds, and he said he'd wanted to talk to me about him. Said the guy had called in earlier as a concerned citizen and told them we're fucking. Said Alex thought that wasn't right seeing as we work together. And he's right, but fucking hell! This Alex guy knows *that* about us? How? We've never shown anything in public, and until earlier we'd never even shown one another. Has he been watching us since this started? Since he followed you as you left Louise's death site?" He slapped the steering wheel. "That's what the wanker's done. He's been keeping tabs on us. Shields said Alex had given him your licence plate number, lied and said he'd seen us kissing outside PrivoLabs."

"That's bullshit. We got straight into the car after we'd been there and drove off."

"I know that, but Shields doesn't. And let's face it, he'd believe anything bad someone said about us. You especially."

"Arsehole can find a cliff and jump the fuck off it."

Langham's rumble of laughter made Oliver smile.

"I love it when you're riled," Langham said.

"Yeah, well, that bloke rubs me up the wrong way."

"I sincerely hope not…"

"Oh, shut the hell up and clean out your filthy mind. Pervert."

They journeyed in silence after that, Oliver thinking on why Langham had got so upset over what Shields knew. Did that mean Langham cared for Oliver more than he'd thought? Were they headed towards more than just a hot and hard fuck, as Langham had put it earlier?

He hoped so, but if he were honest, he'd take whatever Langham gave.

In no time at all, they were driving down Saltwater Street, and the heavy feeling of foreboding made itself known inside Oliver. He tensed—it seemed every muscle in his body hardened. Taking a deep breath, he glanced across at Langham, who frowned at the dilapidated building Mark had described.

"Looks like no one's lived there for years, although there's a light on."

Oliver stared at the house. It was similar to the pub in the hamlet, all wonky walls and concave roof, and he was surprised it still stood, what with the state it was in. It must have been here for over a century—the facade showed serious signs of wear and tear, and the brickwork was rough, not as uniform as the more recently built houses around it. He sighed, trying to shake off the air of oppression in the car, and moved to get out.

Langham grimaced. "If Shields does something about what he's been told… If he makes it known… I'll leave the fucking force before they tell me I can't work with you or try and force me out just because my cock doesn't go in some woman's cunt."

Oliver stared at him, shocked at the vehemence in his words. Langham wasn't against women—far from it, he was polite and respectful—but his word choice in expressing his sexual preferences was so unlike him that Oliver was at a loss for words. How did he answer that?

"I'm sorry," Langham said. "It just makes me see red, that's all. I can fuck a woman, work with her as well at a push, but fuck a man and work with him? Hell no. It's seen as different. Fucked if I know why, fucked if I understand why where I put my dick has any bearing on how I do my job, but there you go. The world is one messed-up place and I'm sick of it."

"It's all right. I understand."

Langham sighed, keeping his gaze ahead. "I won't let them prevent me from having a relationship with you. Not when it's only just started. Before... Shit, it was just a waiting game, a *hoping* game, you know?"

Oliver did know.

"But now?" Langham went on. "No, no bastard's pissing about with my happiness. I'll have it out with that Shields wanker later, but for now we have work to do. Got to focus, because if Alex is in there and he turns nasty?" He paused, then, "We should have back-up, really."

"But we're only asking him where his brother is. We can feel him out and return with extra cops later." Oliver had answered like an automaton—his real thoughts centred on what Langham had just revealed. He wanted to revel in the words, to roll them around in his head and inspect them one by one, but once again this wasn't the time or the place.

"Yeah, but didn't Mark say his brother had turned nasty in a second? That he'd crept up on him or whatever?"

Oliver nodded. "Look, there's two of us. We can question the old lady if you think it would look better, make Alex think we're not there for him in any way. Let's just see how it goes, and if he turns on us...well, we'll deal with it then."

Langham fumbled with his seatbelt, cutting the engine once he'd freed himself. "Fucking mental becoming a cop. Dad always said that. Too much of a risk. Unpredictable people. Yet here I am, walking into something that could be the end of me, taking a damn civilian in with me. Maybe you ought to stay—"

"Fuck you. I am *not* staying in the car. We go in together. Besides, you might need me. I might pick up on something in there."

The detective sighed. "What-fucking-ever. Useless arguing with you."

With both of them out on the pavement, Oliver said, "Come on. Let's get this over and done with."

They walked, heads down, along the path made of broken patio slabs, the cement between crumbling, gone in places. Oliver got a dose of trepidation—it filled him, growing from his toes right to the top of his head, a cold, spiteful fear that left him shaking.

"Something's off here as well, man. Fuck!"

Langham reached the front door first. "Like what? Tell me."

"Like at Mark's place. I don't think Alex is even here." That piece of knowledge eased Oliver's mind somewhat, but the fact that something hinky was going on inside those walls still bothered him. "It isn't clear what's going on in there, but we're going to find more than we bargained for. I feel it. *Know* it."

"All right. Calm down and concentrate. I'll knock, okay?"

Oliver nodded and watched Langham lift a tight fist and bang on the door. Once again, no one answered, and they waited for a moment before Langham knocked again.

"Fucking déjà vu," Langham said, knocking a third time. He walked to the window, another living room Oliver would bet, and held his hands over his eyes to peer inside. "No angry visitors in this one, but the old woman's asleep on the couch."

Oliver knocked—hard and insistent.

"No movement from her," the detective said.

"Probable cause to kick the door down?"

"Yep. I could have thought she was dead, know what I'm saying?"

Oliver nodded, and Langham walked back to the door. It took several kicks to the wood for it to give in and admit them. Langham went first, as always, and rounded the doorframe to their right, entering the room the old lady was in. Caught up in the adrenaline rush of entering a house without permission or a warrant, Oliver didn't catch the sense of a new death. Not until he stood in the centre of the living room behind Langham, whose wide frame blocked Oliver's view of the old woman. He peered around him and recoiled at the sight. She sat on the sofa, head against the back, her mouth filled with those fucking sugar strands, nose held closed with a clothes peg.

Alex was one sick bastard.

"Jesus," Langham breathed, pulling out his radio and calling in her death.

Oliver reversed to the doorway, wanting to put distance between himself and the old lady. He didn't think he could take her spirit latching onto him and spilling the last moments of her life. In the hallway, he waited for Langham to join him, and they followed their usual pattern of scouring the lower and upper rooms before coming back down to stop at a door positioned under the stairs.

"Mark said his brother lived down in the basement, right?" Langham asked.

"Yep. But he isn't down there. I'd say he fucked off once he killed the old woman. But we'd better check anyway, right?"

Langham nodded, opening the only door they hadn't tried. Oliver sighed. Something evil was down there. Langham switched on the light, revealing surprisingly clean plastered walls that turned halfway down. Oliver steeled himself to face whatever it was waiting for them and followed the detective down stairs that creaked every time they stepped on them. The sense of dread grew stronger as they rounded the corner, the light from the stairway giving scant illumination, highlighting only the floor directly before them. The basement could be small or large, for all Oliver knew—the blackness beyond that slice of light hid absolutely everything—and he felt along the wall for another light switch. His fingers brushed over the protruding plastic switch, and he flicked it on.

Sound exploded, like frightened jungle birds, all caws

and startled shrieks. Oliver cursed and jumped, squinting in the burst of light to try to get used to the brightness.

"Oh, fuck me sideways," Langham said, moving forward at speed.

Oliver stared ahead at several cages holding children whose ages ranged from about four through to eight. "Oh my God. I wasn't expecting... I didn't know... Shit!" He walked towards them, smiling to put them at ease, but they continued squawking, their pitch rising, as did their volume. "It's all right. Everything's going to be all right."

Langham fussed with a padlock, trying unsuccessfully to get it open. The children had retreated to the backs of their cages, looking stunned and frightened to death. What the hell were they doing here? Had Alex been hiding them for PrivoLabs? What kind of outfit *were* they, to not have them at least kept secure in a proper environment? Not that keeping them locked up like this was right, but fuck, in a basement? In cages?

A rapid-fire shift of movement caught Oliver's eye, and he saw the kid inside the cage Langham was working on dart forward. "Langham! Watch it!"

Fuck, that child's eyes glowed, the pupils black slits in a circle of lurid yellow. Langham jumped back just before the kid crashed against the cage door, mouth open, teeth gnashing where the detective's hands had so recently been on the padlock.

Langham stepped back, eyes wide. "He was...he was going to *bite* me!"

Oliver's heart hammered, and his legs went weak. They needed to get the hell out of here — and now. Something else was about to go down if they didn't leave this place. Them being down here had clearly upset the kids. Who knew, if they were angry enough, whether they could break out of those cages and attack. He wasn't sure what urged him to grab Langham and propel them up the stairs, but he wasn't about to hang around down there to analyse it.

Out on the street, breaths shunting from them in staccato

bursts, Langham called for back-up. Despite there being kids in that basement, leaving them there didn't make Oliver feel guilty. They weren't kids anymore. They were something…else. Something feral, all humanity stripped out of them by experiments he didn't want to know the ins and outs of. It was all too fucked up to contemplate. The sooner they found Alex, the better, then they could get a warrant to search PrivoLabs and put this hateful case to bed.

Chapter Seven

Shields and other cops had shown up within minutes of Langham making the call. The big, greasy bastard strolled towards them, a smug smile filling his fleshy face as though he thought them a pair of wimps for not remaining in the basement—faggot wimps at that. Yeah, Oliver saw that on his face, too, and he wanted to kick the shit out of the hateful motherfucker for it.

"So there are kids down there, then?" Shields asked.

Stupid of him, really, when Oliver had heard Langham tell him over the phone, but that was just the kind of guy Shields was. Arsehole extraordinaire.

"Kids with glowing eyes," Shields said, not bothering to hide the disbelief in his voice. He raised his hands and waggled his fingers. "Oooh, glowy-eyed kids that fly at you with intent to bite. Nasty business, that. I'll have to go down there and give them a good telling off."

"Be my fucking guest," Langham snarled, striding towards his car. He shouted back, "And if they chew your damn fingers off, don't say I didn't warn you."

He got in his car, and Oliver moved to join him.

"Uh, you stay right there, freak." Shields gripped Oliver's wrist. "You two fucking each other's arses?"

Oliver clenched his teeth, cursing the blush of anger that swarmed over his face. Shields would take it as a sign of embarrassment, of Oliver cowering down to the big man. He wasn't having any of that. "Why? D'you fancy a cock up *your* arse? You asking just in case I'm free with my favours, is that it?"

Shields released Oliver's wrist as though he'd been

tainted by the touch. "Fucking dirty little pervert. Get the fuck away from me."

"Be damn glad to, you nasty bastard. Oh, and watch those kids down there. They're poised to attack."

"Yeah, right. They probably sensed you two are bent. Didn't like it so went for the kill."

"Whatever, arsehole." Oliver walked away, anger at Shields seeping out of him the farther away he got. The moral side of him made Oliver turn to warn the cop again not to go down those stairs, but Shields had already disappeared inside the house. The man wouldn't listen even if he followed him inside and tried to make him take heed. He continued walking, but instead of heading for Langham's car, he approached a cop standing guard on the pavement.

"Shields really shouldn't go down in that basement," he said. "Those kids...they're going to hurt him, but he won't listen to me. Maybe you ought to make sure he doesn't go down alone, make sure he doesn't approach them until medical assistance arrives."

He walked away only when the cop had entered the house. Inside the car, he hooked up his seatbelt and rested his head against the seat.

"Something's going to happen, isn't it?" Langham asked.

"Yep, but you warned him, I warned him and I just sent that cop there to warn him."

"Are we arseholes if we drive away now?"

"Yep, s'pose we would be, but I did all I could, so I refuse to feel bad. He said some nasty shit to me just then. Said some cruel stuff to you on the phone. Okay, he doesn't deserve what he'll get if he goes down those stairs, but fuck, he's so stubborn, so *right* all the damn time, that no amount of pleading from me was going to change his mind. *Especially* pleading from me. He hates my damn guts."

"So we'll stay?"

"Yep."

"Clean up the mess afterwards?"

"Well, I don't know about cleaning up the mess—it's going to be pretty bloody down there if they bite his hands off—but yeah, we'll stay to sort it out."

Langham sighed. "I'm an utter bastard, and I'd only admit this to you, but I want to drive away."

"Then drive."

Langham sped up Saltwater Street, and Oliver refused to think about what could be happening to Shields right then. Sometimes things needed to be left up to fate.

"Where do we go now?" he asked, looking at Langham, who had the facial expression of someone hurt, angry and bewildered all at the same time. "Hey, you okay?"

"I will be once I forget about Shields. He isn't worth wasting thinking time on, but you know what it's like. He gets under your damn skin."

"He does. I wonder if they've bitten him yet."

"Probably."

"He'll be cursing us. That we warned him and he didn't listen."

"Good. A bit of humility won't hurt him. Hey, if we're *really* lucky, the arsehole might even apologise. Act differently towards you."

"I doubt it." And if he were honest, Oliver didn't want Shields admitting he'd been wrong. He didn't want anything more to do with the guy. That wasn't an option, though. Even if he told the chief he and Langham were gay, and they weren't allowed to work together anymore, Oliver would still be called in on cases. Might even be partnered with Shields. He shuddered at the thought. "What will we do if Shields tells?"

"I don't think he will. He likes having people in the palm of his hand. Likes having something over them. We'll do as we're told as long as he keeps threatening us—he knows that."

They lapsed into silence then, and Oliver eyed the scenery.

"Um, I take it we're going to Privo, yeah?"

"Yep."

"To do what?"

"Talk to the manager, the owner, whatever. Tell him we heard rumours, see what he has to say, check out his reaction."

"But wouldn't that be alerting him? Letting him know we're onto him?"

"It'll be all over the news shortly anyway. No way those kids being found can be contained. Someone will leak it to the press. Better we get to Privo before the owner sees the news and gets his story straight before we get to him."

"Ah, so you *can* be a detective after all. You don't really need me." Oliver smiled, awaiting a sarcastic response.

"Fuck you, man."

"Tonight?" Oliver flushed at his forwardness. That one word had tumbled out before he'd got his brain into gear.

"Uh, are you serious or fucking me about?"

Bolder now, Oliver said, "I'll *fuck* you about, if you like. Any time." *Where the hell did that come from?*

Langham momentarily lost control of the car, and it swerved to the middle of the road. "Shit, don't tell me stuff like that when I'm driving!"

"Sorry."

"You will be. Especially if we crash and you break another finger."

Oliver absently rubbed the bandage keeping his broken finger strapped to the one beside it. It ached like a motherfucker, but he hadn't had much time to feel sorry for himself or wallow in the pain.

"My brother came for lunch."

"Pardon?" Oliver said, unsure whether he'd heard the voice in his head right.

Langham sighed. "I said you will be if we crash and you break—"

"No, I wasn't talking to you."

"Right. Okay, I'll keep quiet." Langham gripped the wheel tighter.

Oliver prayed Mark hadn't just managed to make a

connection with one lousy sentence that told him jack shit. He closed his eyes and waited.

"My brother. Alex came to lunch where I work. I'm – I was an accountant. That's why… Louise, that's her name… That's why Louise was filing, why she found the notes. They were in PrivoLabs' papers. She showed them to me, and I rang Privo, let them know we had something that didn't belong in their account file."

"And?"

"I went back to work and did a bit of digging. Asked this lab technician I know at Privo to keep an eye out, see what was going on. Told him what was on the note. He said it was about a new drug he'd been testing. That it wasn't ready yet."

"Oh, God."

"Next day, some guy I hadn't seen before, from Privo, turned up when I was eating lunch in the courtyard outside my work with Alex. The guy, he said he needed the note, and I gave it to him – had it in my inside pocket, didn't I. Anyway, after he'd gone, Alex started asking questions. I told him what the note had said, what the lab guy said, and…"

"And what?"

"He wanted to blackmail them. Said he'd make some money out of them. That he'd threaten to go to the papers. So after he left, I went back inside and rang the lab technician again, but…"

"But what? Mark? Mark? Shit. You still there? Tell me what happened then?"

"I guess they got to Alex. Fed him those meds."

"Yeah, that much is pretty damn obvious. Fuck, I didn't mean that to sound so nasty. Who's the technician?"

"Ronan Dougherty, lives in the flats above the corner shop on Kater Road, but I can't – couldn't – get hold of him. His phone rang off the hook."

"Fuck."

"I think – "

"Yep, me too."

"Alex…"

"Yep, he's probably paid the tech a visit already."

"He wasn't like that before. Not mean like he is now."

Oliver shielded his thoughts. If Alex was willing to resort to blackmail, he wasn't your average kind of guy. Anyone who could hatch a plan pretty damn quick like that and go off to make it happen… Yeah, Alex was a bad lot, no mistaking that—the drugs had just made him worse. Privo had him under their control, offing everyone who knew about what they were doing. It was only a matter of time before Alex got to him and Langham.

"Anything else?" he asked Mark.

Silence.

"Mark?" Oliver waited.

No response.

"Well?" Langham demanded.

"We're next on the damn list. Got to be."

"What, Alex's list?"

"Yeah, and after we've been to Privo, we need to go back to Louise's field. Mark's body is still there, remember?"

Langham handed Oliver the radio. "Sorry to do this to you, but ask for Shields. If he can't come to the phone, we know he's been bitten."

Oliver stifled a smirk. "So I'm telling him, or whoever, where Mark is?"

"Yeah, make out you've only just been told. If they find out about the time lapse, we're fucked."

He made the call, was put through to Shields, who never mentioned whether the kids had got to him or not. He wouldn't want to lose face, but they'd know soon enough. Shields said he'd head over to the field now and asked that Langham report to him once they'd been to Privo.

Oliver put the radio back on its clip and asked Langham, "Why did Shields ask that you report to him? He's not above you in command, is he, so…?"

"Like I said, he wants people in his pocket. He knows I'll know exactly what he means by telling me to report to him. It's a game to him, but for fuck's sake, it's our damn *lives* he's fucking with. Emotions."

"Doubt he'd know what they even were, emotions. Don't reckon he has any. Not loving ones anyway."

"You might be right there. Come on, we're here. Time to question whoever's in charge of this fucked-up place."

Inside the building, Oliver expected to feel some familiarity, but he didn't. The plants had gone—some soil was still scattered around the base of the pots—and one sofa was missing. He glanced at Langham, who had noted the change too, and they walked up to the desk.

The receptionist looked at them with fear in her eyes, and her mouth worked like she wanted to tell them something but struggled to get the words out. "C-can I help you?"

"We need to speak with the owner, the director. The person in charge here."

"Mr Jackson isn't available at the moment. We had a…" She stared ahead at the space where the sofa had been. "An unhappy visitor an hour ago, so Mr Jackson is… indisposed."

"Indisposed in what way?" Langham asked, producing his badge. "Is he ill? Not here?"

"No, he's here, but he said—"

"I don't care what he said. I need to speak to him."

The receptionist widened her eyes at Langham's tone and maintained eye contact as she reached out for the phone. She dialled without looking at the keypad and jumped when someone answered. "S-sorry. Yes, I know you said… There are detectives here." She eyed them keenly. "Yes, that's them… Oh, right. Well, I'll send them up, then."

Oliver's stomach muscles tautened. He wasn't stupid. Mr Jackson had described them to her, knew they'd be on their way, that a visit from them was due. This didn't bode well, and if the push inside his brain was anything to go by, spirits were trying to warn him that something wasn't right.

"Mr Jackson will see you now," she said, pasting on a fake smile. "Use the elevator. Top floor, the only office up there."

"Thank you," Langham said, striding towards the double silver doors of the elevator. He jabbed the button and tapped his foot.

Oliver smiled at the receptionist before joining the detective, whispering, "He knows."

"Yep." Langham flexed his jaw.

"How are we going to play this?"

"Don't speak." He stepped inside the elevator and glanced up into the top corner.

Oliver followed him and his gaze. A camera studied them.

"Right," Langham said, clearing his throat. "We'll alert Mr Jackson about the ridiculous rumours circulating about his company, then we'll go to that corner shop where we got those microwave curries from before, you know where I mean?"

Oliver got the gist—the lab tech's flat—and nodded. "Yep, been a long day. I'm starving. Pick up some beer too."

"Sounds good." Langham sighed. "I hate having to bring this kind of information to someone. The potential those rumours have to ruin a company doesn't bear thinking about. Malicious, that's what people are."

"Too right."

The elevator came to a perfect, gliding stop, and the doors slid open. A huge space met them, an open-plan office that took up the whole floor. Several desks were dotted about, but only one was occupied. It was situated rear centre, shielded from the others either side by black zigzag screens. A man sat behind the desk, head bent, giving them the impression that he was hard at work and had nothing to hide, thank you very much.

Langham cleared his throat again, and the man looked up.

"Mr Jackson?" Langham asked.

The man stood, rounding his desk and strolling towards them with the air of someone who was at ease with who he was. His dark grey suit—pressed so well that his trousers still bore the strict line down the front despite the fact that the man had possibly been sitting for untold hours—fitted him just right. No pulling material on broad shoulders here, or a tight waistband. This guy took care of his body. Shoulder-length wavy hair, that strange colour between brown and black, made Oliver think of Antonio Banderas in his eighties days.

"Ah, hello, Detectives," Jackson said.

Langham didn't correct him, and Oliver felt stupidly proud that he could pass as a member of the police force.

"What can I do for you?" Jackson walked towards his desk, looking back over his shoulder with eyebrows raised as though asking if they wanted to follow him.

They did, and at the desk, after they were all seated, Langham said, "I'm sorry to bother you with this, but we thought it best we told you personally. Rumours are circulating about your company doing experiments on children—and on a man named Alex Reynolds. Of course, this is utterly ridiculous, but we felt you should know in case something unfortunate hits the news later tonight."

Jackson abruptly sat straighter, covering his slip of alarm by making out he was reaching for a pen and notebook. He held them in hands that didn't shake, held their gaze too, an unwavering stare that spoke of him being calm and collected now. Clever bastard. "Really? How on earth did you come by this information?"

Langham rolled his eyes. "Some children were found in the basement at Alex Reynolds' home. If he's to be believed, your company has been conducting experiments on them."

"Experiments on children? That's a little far-fetched, don't you think?" Jackson did the flabbergasted look well.

"Indeed," Langham said. "Between you and me, we think Reynolds is trying to hide the fact he had the children down there for…*other* reasons."

"Oh, God. That's disgusting." Jackson put his pen and pad down.

"People will do anything to get themselves out of trouble, sir." Langham smiled sheepishly, as though it was his fault

Reynolds had spun such a tale. "But we wanted you aware. If it leaks out what he's said… I don't have to tell you the devastating effects this could have on your company. Even if he's lying, people will remember the PrivoLab name for all the wrong reasons."

"Well, thank you for coming to tell me. I'll alert my staff and let them know we have a 'no comment' policy should they be approached by the press."

"Very sensible." Langham paused. "So, you wouldn't object if we asked to take a look around? Specifically at your labs."

"Of course not. I'll take you on a tour immediately."

"Very good, sir. It's for the best. I can radio in to my chief once we've had a look about and let him know the rumours are totally unfounded — he's expecting us to call him in half an hour or so. Hopefully, if we're quick, I can get that information to him before the news airs. Perhaps he'll be able to telephone the newsroom and let them know he's available for comment. It can only help your company."

Jackson stood quickly. "Yes, yes. I'll show you around right now."

Chapter Eight

"Well, that was a waste of time," Oliver grumbled as they sat in the car in the delivery area out the back of PrivoLabs.

A massive bush, which had protested with a groan of branches and the spiteful scratch of thorns on car paintwork as Langham had reversed into it, shielded them from view. Of course, Jackson could have seen them hiding the car in his shrubbery, but then again, he may well have been too intent on covering his arse to have bothered looking out of the window at whether they drove away or not. Maybe Langham's ruse had worked, put Jackson at ease. Perhaps the guy had believed him.

"I'm not qualified to know what the fuck we were looking for," Oliver went on, "and any drugs they had on the shelves looked the same as any I can get over the counter in the damn supermarket. And you do realise he's going to dump any drugs relating to those kids now, don't you?"

"He won't. They cost too much. Shit, the leaves are seriously thick. I can't see much except the back door of the place."

"Fuck the back door!"

"I will once this pissing case is over!" Langham bit back.

"I thought we were fucking tonight."

"Yeah, we are. Look, shut the hell up while I concentrate."

"And you say *I'm* a bitch?"

Oliver didn't push it further, knew to keep quiet now. Their banter had no place when Langham was uptight and staking out.

"He'll call someone, you'll see." Langham leant forward, squinted to see through the foliage covering the windscreen.

"They'll come and collect the drugs and anything related to them."

"And I take it we'll follow."

"Yeah."

"So what about visiting Ronan Dougherty's flat? Seeing if he's been cut up, has arms missing like Mark? See if those strands are all over him?"

"Shit!" Langham whacked the steering wheel, narrowly missing blasting the horn. "What the hell is wrong with me? I forgot about him. Call it in to Shields, same deal as before—you've only just been told. Tell him what we're doing too."

Oliver obeyed, wincing at the sound of Shields' smarmy voice coming at him over the airwaves.

"I told you to tell *Langham* to report to me," Shields barked. "Not you, freak. What's he doing that has him so tied up he can't speak to me?"

"He's the one who'll be driving, following the people, if they come to collect the drugs." Oliver closed his eyes, willing himself not to snap back, but his mouth worked before he could stop it. "Why, did you want to taunt him about being bent again, is that it? Hey, why don't you say what you have to say to me? I mean, I'm a freaky fag, too, so you'll hit home with either one of us. Doesn't matter which one you speak to."

"Fuck off, you little spirit-hearing bastard."

"Ah, so you admit I *do* hear them, then? That it isn't *me* killing these people?"

Shields spluttered. "No, no, that's not it at all. I still think it's you. That you have a gang, some guys who kill when you're with Langham so it just *looks* like it isn't you."

"Oh, give me a fucking break, shithead."

Langham lifted his eyebrows at that, smiled then continued studying ahead.

"Shithead? Fuck, I'll have the chief take you off civilian duty for that. You shouldn't even be with Langham now. Probably had a quick fuck in those bushes, haven't you."

75

"And I'll speak to the chief about your disgusting mouth and the crap you come out with. You do know gays are accepted in the force now, don't you? Like, they can be openly gay. I mean, words in the right ears could cost you your job. You're victimising us."

Shields laughed, hard and rough. "Prove it, freak."

"These calls are monitored at random, aren't they? Recorded? I could get Langham to call someone now so they make sure to listen to this call once we're done, if you like?"

Shields remained quiet for several seconds. "Just let me know if something goes down."

"Oh, I will do. You want me to tell you if something happens at Privo too?"

"What the hell are you on about? Yes, of course I do! That's what I just said!"

"Well, it's just that you said about something going down, and off the back of our conversation before, about being gay and all, I thought you were referring to *me* going down on Langham." Oliver struggled to hold back his laughter.

"You dirty little bastard. You know damn well what I meant. Just call it in."

Oliver re-hooked the radio and let out a stream of laughter. *Fuck, that felt good to get back at that greasy wanker.* "There. I think your job is safe now, don't you? And I reckon we'll still be working together."

Langham quickly glanced at him then back at the Privo building. "Jesus, I knew you were a mouthy little sod, but I didn't think you had it in you to bite back at Shields."

"He's pissed me off long enough. Besides, he started messing with you. I won't have that."

Langham looked at him again, his expression tender. "Why did we wait so long?"

"I don't know. Fear of rejection, I guess."

"Yeah." He looked away again. "Fuck, mushy moment over. Someone's here. Hand me the camera, quick!"

Oliver fumbled in the glovebox and pulled the digital

camera out. He switched it on. "Careful, battery's low."

"Always forget to charge the bloody thing. Thanks."

A large white truck backed into the Privo yard, reverse alarm bleeping. Once the truck had stopped, four men dressed head to toe in black poured out of the cab and approached the back door. It opened, and Jackson appeared in the doorway, head darting left to right as he inspected the area. Obviously deeming it safe, he ushered the men inside and closed the door.

"You catch all that?" Oliver asked.

"Yep. Got some good close-ups too. Keep your eye on the door. Let me know when they come out again. I'm just going to check the pictures I took." He glanced down at them then switched the camera off. He reached for his radio. "I'm going to need back-up."

He relayed into the radio that unmarked cars needed to be at the rear of Privo for when Langham and Oliver followed the truck when it left. Whether that meant those cops would go in and arrest Mr Jackson, or wait to follow him in case *he* left, Oliver didn't know. He had no time to contemplate further either – the black-clad men were coming out of the back door, loading boxes into the truck.

"Langham..."

The detective looked up. "So he does have something to hide. Bastard."

They sat in silence, watching, Oliver losing count of the boxes once they went over fifty. That was some serious amount of drugs there. Maybe the shit they'd used to make them too. Everything was evidence these days. Oliver imagined Jackson panicking, wondering how the hell he could cover his bases, ensuring that those workers oblivious to what he'd really been doing with those drugs still only thought they'd been working on something innocent. Who knew, maybe the guy would just announce he'd pulled the plug on their research, that the drug wasn't viable, too expensive to produce, something like that. Whatever he did, he'd have to do it fast. Just by Langham snapping pictures of the guy letting the men into Privo had him banged to rights for *some* kind of crime. Aiding and abetting. Whatever. So long as the man went down for a stretch and the killings stopped, Oliver would be happy.

"Hold up," Langham said. "They're on the fucking move." He barked into his radio that back-up ought to get here pretty damn quick.

The truck rumbled to life, Jackson standing at the back door as the vehicle eased forward and nosed out onto the main road. Then he closed the door, the truck joined the light traffic and Langham took the opportunity to start his car and follow. The branches had a jolly time scratching the paintwork again, and Oliver glanced to the side to see Langham's reaction. The detective winced.

There were only two cars between Langham's and the truck, and they tailed it at an acceptable thirty miles per hour. No bringing attention to themselves. No smart-arse overtaking to get closer. The truck was large enough to be seen for a good few hundred yards ahead, so providing they remained on this straight road for a while, they didn't risk losing it.

The two cars turned right, stalling Langham and Oliver for a few seconds. Oliver's heart rate increased, adrenaline speeding through him too fast for comfort. He felt sick, had never been on a pursuit before and had no idea what Langham had in mind. Would they just follow until the truck had reached its destination? If they did, didn't they risk being spotted if the end of their journey was in some remote place?

"What's next?" he asked, noting the truck had turned left onto the slip road leading to the motorway.

"We follow, see where it goes."

"So we don't flag it down, get them to stop?"

"Not at the moment, no. There are too many men inside for me to deal with should they turn nasty. Got to wait for that goddamn silent radio to squawk and let me know *we're* being followed by other cops. I could pull them over on a random truck check, ask to look inside, and then what? If we find those damn strands, yep, we'd have reason to take the men in, but like I said, one of me, four of them. They're not likely to go with me without a fight. Looked a nasty set of bastards, didn't they."

Oliver agreed. Big, burly men they wouldn't stand a chance against. "Obvious they've got the drugs in the back."

"Of course they have. Forensics will have a field day finding out what those strands contain. Wonder if they've got around to doing those from Louise's body yet?" He snorted. "Doubt it. They're way behind with evidence processing. Always are. You'd think there'd be more employed. For times like this, when we need a quick analysis in order to bring someone in. We need solid proof the strands on Louise and in that old woman's mouth are the same ones in the truck. And those they'll find on Mark's body."

"Wonder if Shields has arrived there yet. And I wonder what they're going to do with those kids. How they'll get them out without being bitten or attacked."

"Only thing I can think of is drugging them, and that doesn't sit well with me, seeing as they're drugged up to the fucking eyeballs already. Poor little bastards."

Oliver thought of their parents, frantic with worry for however long their children had been missing. Of the police, busy now matching each child to every missing persons report. Visiting those parents. Breaking the news that their previously cute little one had possibly killed. "Fuck, this is such a mess."

"It is. Bet you wish you didn't hear voices now, don't you."

Oliver nodded. He didn't need to answer verbally. Didn't want to. If he did, everything he felt inside would tumble out. Like how he'd coped with this all his life, borne the ridicule of his family for being such a freak. God knows how they'd have taken it if he'd told them he was gay as well. Heart Attack City, he suspected. Did they see him in the newspapers, on the news, as the same freak? Or did they now wish they'd been more understanding? He was famous, kind of. People knew his face, stopped him sometimes, shouted insults at others. Fuck, he just wanted to live a quiet life, but fate had had other things in mind from the day he was damn well born.

He sighed, gusting out a breath full of resignation. He was stuck as he was whether he liked it or not. Couldn't ignore the voices any more than he could choose not to breathe. It just wasn't happening.

"You okay?" Langham asked, glancing over with a look of concern.

"Yeah, was just thinking."

"Of?"

"The past. Now. The future."

"In what way?"

The truck took another slip road, one that rose up to join an overpass.

"Me, being the way I am. Wishing I wasn't. Wishing I was normal."

"Fuck, and my question brought that up for you. Sorry."

"It's okay. Nothing I don't think about by myself from time to time anyway. I mean, it's hardly something you can ignore, is it. I could go to some channeller, get them to teach me to tune the dead out, but I'd only beat myself up over who the spirits could turn to then."

"Catch-22."

"Yep."

"Look," Langham said, pointing out the windshield. "The truck's heading towards Lingbrough."

Oliver peered ahead. "Figures. If they stop there, unload somewhere, wouldn't surprise me. Quiet village. Houses few and far between. Not the type of place to be spotted by a nosey community. Heard that place has snobs living there. No one wanting to be friendly with anyone else."

"Perfect hideout."

"Yeah." Oliver glanced back to see if they were being

followed. They were, by a beat-up, old-style Ford Escort van, a nineties job that looked as though it'd be better off on the scrap heap. A *red* van. His guts bunched. "Your undercover back-up tend to drive red rust buckets?"

"No." Langham stared in the rear-view mirror for a second. "Fuck. Reckon that's Alex Reynolds?"

"Who the fuck knows. This is the first time I've been involved directly with one of your cases so I don't know how this shit works. Find the body, report to you and go home, that's me. I don't get to see all this bullshit usually. But, not being a total thicko, I can see how it probably is him. How Jackson might have called him to tail the truck. So now he's going to know we're onto them."

"Just thought the same myself. If Alex has been watching us like I think he has, he'd have already clocked my car way before now. So Jackson will also know what we're up to. Fucking great."

Oliver looked back again. "No sign of any other cars behind the van either."

Langham snatched up the radio, asking where the fuck back-up was. Told three miles behind. "Well, they ought to put their foot down on the pedal, then, because we've got Alex Reynolds on our tail." He hooked the radio back on the dash and said, "I don't fancy him behind doing the same to us as he did to you when you'd found Louise. Wouldn't put it past him either. Fucking wig, mask and all. Those weird eyes his brother told you about."

Mark Reynolds had said Alex hadn't acted like he usually did. Those drugs had a lot to answer for. As did the man who had ordered them to be made and distributed with intent to make people kill. Jackson. What a fucking arsewipe. Another thought hit him then. Maybe Jackson was just a middle man, the one with the means to make the drugs. What if someone else had approached *him* with the drugging idea? Someone with a shitload of power who wasn't to be ignored if you knew what was good for you?

He huffed out a long breath, the air vibrating between

his lips making them tingle. This was way bigger than he'd imagined, and being here now in the thick of it didn't seem such a good idea. Yet he'd insisted he was tagging along with Langham to every lead. For some reason, this case had got to him more than the others — maybe because Louise had contacted him *while* she'd been being killed and not after.

He didn't get to ponder that further. Alex pulled alongside them.

And rammed his van into the side of Langham's car.

"Oh fuck, not again," Oliver said, leaning forward to stare out of Langham's side window at Alex. "This bloke is fucking *mental*."

"There are a lot of them about," Langham said, holding tight to the wheel to keep the vehicle on the road. He glanced sideward, then gunned the accelerator, gaining a car-length's space between their back and his front. "And they don't tend to give up easily."

Langham's statement was proved true with a shunt to the rear of his car. Oliver pitched forward, flung his hands out to brace himself on the dash. His broken finger throbbed at the contact, and he grimaced.

"If that bastard breaks another of my fingers, or something else of mine, including you, I'll kill the fucker."

"By the looks of things, he's going to give it a good go." Langham drove faster, almost catching up to the truck. "I'd better move, in case the truck is ordered to stop and we go up its arse, Alex going up ours. I don't fancy being inside a concertina sandwich, do you?"

"Not really, no."

Oliver closed his eyes, praying this would all end soon — with good results. Relief poured into him at the sound of sirens, and he looked through the back window to see that help had arrived, that other officers had finally got their arses into gear and put some speed into their pursuit. Four unmarked vehicles followed, one overtaking Alex to slip between Langham's car and his, two boxing him in either side, and one at the rear. Langham glanced in the rear-view and, seeing Alex was taken care of, breathed out his own relief.

"So now what?" Oliver said, hoping the back-up would also take care of the truck.

"We carry on following them," the detective said, nodding ahead.

Shit.

Chapter Nine

After Langham had driven around for a couple of minutes to throw the truck driver off the fact that they'd been following them, and had almost been run off the road by Alex, once again, Langham wedged his car inside some high-as-a-house bushes, one of the back-up vehicles beside them. As they sat observing a large house situated in expansive grounds down a lane just off the motorway, awaiting further back-up, Oliver took a moment to calm down. News had come via one of the officers in the next car that Alex Reynolds had been apprehended, a clawing, insane mass of anger that had taken six officers to subdue. Oliver was glad it hadn't been up to them to arrest him— fucked if he would have been able to help Langham without shitting himself. He wasn't a softy, but something like that was way out of his comfort zone. He was only human, after all, and with no training under his belt, he'd have been more hindrance than help. It could have all ended so differently too. Alex could have turned weird-eyed on them and killed their arses.

He shuddered and took the binoculars Langham handed across to him.

"You have a turn. My eyes are crossing."

Oliver peered through them, momentarily freaked by the closeness of what he saw. The truck was parked directly outside the house, a sprawling monstrosity that spoke of high maintenance and a shedload of cash. The men were nowhere to be seen, no doubt inside, secreting the drugs and whatever the hell else they'd removed from Privo. The cops en route were trained to get inside and round the inhabitants up, secure the truck and its contents, and Oliver thanked fuck for that.

Langham's mobile rang, startling Oliver so the binoculars banged his brow bone. He lowered them, rubbing the sore spot, and glanced at the caller display. Shields. He smiled as Langham jabbed the speakerphone button.

"Yep?" Langham closed his eyes for a second, probably steeling himself for whatever the other detective had to say.

"Langham?"

"Who else?"

"Wasn't sure if your *friend* there would be answering. You still outside the house?"

"Yep."

"The team not arrived yet?"

"Obviously not, otherwise I wouldn't be here."

"As soon as they do, I need you back here."

"What for? Can't you cope with Ronan Dougherty's flat and Mark Reynolds' site by yourself?" Langham rolled his eyes and smirked.

"Not amusing, Langham. That's sorted. Dougherty's dead, as you suspected. Arms hacked off, face slashed. Mark Reynolds. Dead. In the field like *your man* said. Officers are dealing with it all now."

"So? What do you want?"

"Like I said. You. Back here."

Oliver was feeling all kinds of irritation, so God knew what Langham felt. Langham clenched his teeth and drummed his fingers on his thigh.

"Paperwork?" Langham asked.

"You wish," Shields said, his oily tone grating yet slick at the same time. "No, we've got another couple of bodies. Different to the others."

"Shit. So there's someone else out there. Unless Alex offed them before he followed us, changed the way he does things to throw us off."

"He's too up himself to do that," Shields said. "He'd have wanted us to know it was him, that he was one step ahead.

In control. No, this is an amateur. A bloody messy one at that. And I know who the hell we're looking for, too."

Oliver suspected Shields wanted Langham to beg for the answer. Wanted them both to know he was in the lead now, the one dishing out orders.

"Right," Langham said. "Won't be long. The team will be here in a minute. It'll take us about twenty to get back. Where do you need us?"

"'Us'? No, I need *you*."

Langham sighed, but quietly, so Shields couldn't hear. "Oliver comes with me."

"That's disgusting."

"Very funny, Shields, but that's your filthy mind talking. You know what I meant, and like Oliver said, if you keep making innuendoes…"

"Right. I need you at fifty-four Bridgewater Road, back in the city. Soon as you can. You have to see this scene to believe it. It'll give you an idea of just what we're dealing with."

"What? Don't you mean who?"

"Well, yeah, it's a who *and* a what. A damn demon, if you ask me. Can't have been right in the head before she took the drugs."

"She? Jesus…"

"Yeah, she. A four-foot, pigtailed blonde."

"You've seen her? Know her?"

"Yep, I've seen her. She's one of those damn kids from Alex's basement. Gave an officer the slip just before they made it to the police van that'd take them to hospital. Feisty little bitch, too."

"Fuck. This just keeps getting better."

"Yeah, well. Nothing we can do but find her before she kills someone else. And when you get here, you'll see how much she enjoys it too."

* * * *

Oliver stood beside Langham on the pavement outside fifty-four Bridgewater Road. A sense of desolation took over him. This wasn't your average home. Just looking at the state of it told him that. Snot-smeared windows, where kids had been staring outside, or maybe they had a dog who relished slobbering on glass. A front door with red peeling paint, the letterbox rust-spotted, the numbers five and four wonky beside it. Unkempt garden, abundant with weeds and household debris — a TV with a smashed screen and a chest of drawers with the handles missing. A supermarket shopping trolley too.

Jesus Christ.

He imagined the homes either side would lean away from their companion if they hadn't been part of a terrace. The stench wafting out of the open front door was enough to put anyone off entering. Age-old shit and urine, over-cooked cabbage, all combined into an aroma that almost had Oliver gagging. And this was winter. He couldn't even begin to imagine the smell in high summer.

Shields barrelled towards them, out of the house and down the cracked concrete path, a white handkerchief pressed to his nose. Oliver took a minute to enjoy the man's obvious distress.

"Oh, Jesus," Shields said, blinking rapidly and stuffing the hanky in his suit pocket. "Not only is that a horrendous kill, but that *house*..." He shuddered, swallowed, his Adam's apple bobbing. "Looks like no one *ever* cleaned."

"Tell me what you know. About the girl," Langham said.

"Abused kid, by all accounts. Neighbours say she wasn't looked after properly. Didn't need them to tell me that. Stayed up all hours, left alone most of the time while the parents were out on the piss. And when they were home they were pissed then too. Damn shame. Neighbours hadn't even been aware she was missing, just assumed she'd been kept off school like she had in the past, not allowed out, that kind of thing."

Shields took in a large breath, his facial expression

showing he fully expected the air to be rank. When it wasn't—or evidently not as bad as it was inside—he smiled with relief.

"Parents report her missing?" Langham eyed the house with a critical eye, tic flickering beneath it.

"No. Apparently, the girl—"

"She have a name?"

"Yes, Glenn Close. Can you believe that? She turned into a bunny boiler just like her namesake too."

Oliver wondered how Shields could joke like that. Yeah, he knew cops had to, in order to get through the day, the horrific things they dealt with, but Oliver's heart had been twisted with the knowledge that drugs had made this little girl commit murder. That her life had been one of neglect and without love prior to her taking those drugs, only for her to be catapulted into a different kind of horror. Poor kid.

"Go on," Langham urged, clearly impatient. He tapped his foot, ran a rigid hand through his hair.

"So, if the neighbours are to be believed, Glenn—still can't get over that—had run away before. Returned after a day or two. Maybe her parents assumed this time was the same."

"Maybe they didn't care," Oliver said.

Shields ignored him. "So, that's her background. No other family except those in that house. No friends. And no one knows where she went when she did go missing. Social Services were aware of her, but you know their policy—best to keep the child with her mother for as long as they can, even if that mother's off her face half the time."

"Heard about that myself," Oliver said. "The wrench of separation is apparently far worse for the kid than placing her in a nice home where someone gives a shit. Makes no sense to me. Children can adapt. She'd have got over it, had a better life. Now?" He couldn't finish what he'd wanted to say. The thought of where Glenn would end up should she be caught didn't bear thinking about. A damaged soul forever, most likely, always thinking she was in the wrong, that no one cared.

Shields stared at him like he'd spoken out of turn, and also like Oliver was a piece of shit he was tolerating only because of their threat to expose his harassment of them. He turned away, looked at Langham. "So, when you go inside, you'll understand the mess you'll see."

They followed Shields up the path. Ordinarily, Oliver would have entertained shoving the man forward so he tripped, and he laughed to himself about the imagery, but he was fucked if he could do that now. Emotions gripped him—those of whoever had been killed inside—and they weren't pretty.

"Fucking little bitch. Knew I shouldn't have had her. Was going to get an abortion, wasn't I? But my old man reckoned it'd be a laugh to have a kid. Social Security payments would go up. So I had her, and look where it got us."

Oliver stopped walking, held his hand up to alert Langham that the dead had spoken. "Where is she?"

"Don't know, don't fucking care."

Langham stopped too, waving at Shields to do the same. The smarmy detective gave an eye roll and huffed out an impatient breath. But he halted.

"You don't have any idea where she might have gone?" Oliver asked.

"No. Well, maybe. Made a pal for herself with some old biddy down the road. Reckon that's where she fucked off to when she disappeared for days on end. Pissed me off, that did. Had no one here to make my cuppas."

Oliver bit down on his tongue. He wanted to rip this woman a new arsehole. Her cackling laugh, rich with phlegm, churned his stomach.

"Down this road?"

"Yeah. Number ninety-seven. Mrs Roosay. Some poncy name like that."

Oliver couldn't hold his anger back any longer. "And it didn't *bother* you? You just let your child go there without checking the woman out *first?"*

"Course I fucking didn't. Why would I? Got her out from under my feet, didn't it?"

He couldn't resist his retort. "But your cuppas…"

"Yeah, there was that, but I wasn't too fussed. Not really. Wouldn't be long before someone else would be there to do it."

"What do you mean?"

"Nosey bastard, aren't you?"

She cackled again, the sound fading, and Oliver knew he'd lost her.

"Shit." He pinched the bridge of his nose, a headache threatening to lay him out. "She's gone. Didn't offer much except the fact Glenn visited with an old lady at number ninety-seven. A Mrs Roosay."

Shields lifted onto his tiptoes, peering down the street. "That's down there. Come inside here first, Langham, then you can take your lapdog down there and interview the neighbour." He shook his head. "I knocked on that door too. Thought she was out."

Oliver was too weary to snipe back about the lapdog comment. His energy had been sapped by Glenn's mother, leaving behind the taint of evil and utter disregard for anyone but herself. He sighed as they stepped into the house, mentally preparing himself for what he was about to see. He hoped to God that woman wouldn't contact him again once he stood by her body.

"In here," Shields said, leading them through a doorway in the hall and into a lounge. He stood in the centre, looking to his left, and out came the handkerchief again.

Langham joined him, and by the look on his face, Oliver wasn't sure he wanted to follow. Langham had paled, his lips were drawn back in a grimace and the frown that appeared gouged deep crevices in his brow.

Oliver went into the room.

Glenn's mother was an unrecognisable heap of innards, legs and arms protruding from it. Intestines, heart, lungs, kidneys and her liver mounded high inside a ripped-open torso that had bled profusely. The air had dried them out a little, darkened them, but the carnage wasn't something you could imagine. It had to be seen to be believed.

"Where's her head?" Oliver whispered.

"Over here," Shields said, the words muffled by his hanky.

Oliver followed Shields' pointed finger. The head sat in the corner of the room, wedged on top of a pile of scrunched-up newspaper and oily fish and chip wrappers. An upended fast-food-joint cup lay beside it, and there was a note beside that.

"What's the note say?" Oliver asked.

"Kid's writing, bit of an angry scrawl but legible," Shields said. "It says, '*Here's your fucking tea*'. I assume the cup had tea in it, judging by the darker stain on the carpet around the neck stump, but it's difficult to tell, what with the amount of blood."

Oliver allowed himself a small smile at the sense of victory Glenn must have felt then. He didn't condone killing of any kind, but in this situation… No, he wasn't going to go there.

"There's something else too." Shields pointed to the opposite corner. "Another note as well."

Oliver dared himself to turn his head. What looked like a foetus lay curled in the corner, a filthy, ragged blanket over it, only the head poking out.

"And *that* note?" Langham asked.

Shields moved to the door behind Oliver. "Says, '*I saved you from doing it*'."

Oliver pushed past Shields and went out into the hallway, his mind swimming with what Glenn must have put up with for her to have killed her mother knowing she was pregnant. Her logic in killing her unborn sibling wasn't lost on him. She'd saved the child a life of hell like she'd had. Christ, she must have suffered so much, harboured so much rage, and the drugs had given her the impetus to erase it all. Except it would be in her mind, lingering. Always. He understood why it was such a rage killing. Drugged up and crazed Glenn might be, but somewhere inside was a little girl who just wanted to be loved and accepted.

It sickened Oliver. All of it.

"There's another one." Shields walked past Oliver, making a show of ensuring they didn't touch in the small space, and began walking upstairs.

Langham followed, his expression grim. Oliver had wanted Langham to look at him, to allow him to offer an understanding smile or some other way to show that he was aware of what *his man* was going through. But he hadn't been able to. Langham took the stairs one at a time, arms heavy by his sides, as though every ounce of energy had been sucked out of him. Oliver felt the same, and when he trailed the two detectives, his legs felt like they'd give way any minute and he'd tumble back down, landing in the filth of the hallway, stinky old shoes and a broken tennis racquet for a pillow.

On the landing, one strewn with dirty laundry, bursting refuse sacks — he was surprised this household even owned any or knew what they were — and an odd assortment of bric-a-brac, he breathed in through his mouth. The whole house was filled with the stench of death, cloying and thick, making him want to cough his guts up and run out into the fresh air. But he wanted to be with Langham every step of the way on this case, and if it meant viewing another corpse then so be it.

Inside the box bedroom, a man sat on a bare mattress stained by his blood and who only knew what else. Dark stains, light stains — piss and shit most likely — and patches of crusty dirt that may well have been mud or food. He wasn't sure and didn't much want to entertain it further. The body held his gaze then. Sitting up like that, he looked for all the world like a normal guy, just taking a nap in the nude. His eyes were closed, his hands clasped over his beach ball belly and his black hair flopped forward over one eye. Both legs stuck out in front of him, the backs of his knees touching the mattress edge, the heels of his feet on a matted rug.

But he no longer owned a penis. It sat beside him, holding down a note like an obscene paperweight. Blood had dripped from it, leaving a dribble that had meandered across the page, a now black-encrusted river.

She'd cut it off when he'd been alive, then.

But how had she killed him? Nothing else appeared out of place. Just a guy napping, sans dick.

Shields broke their shocked silence, his voice overly abrasive. Perhaps the thought of losing *his* cock like that had got to him. Oliver almost smiled.

"This note says, '*Hope you enjoyed your dinner.*' Seems obvious the girl had cooked for them, been a skivvy. She must have fed him something. Won't know what that was until the coroner's had a good look at him and the tox screens come back."

Langham cleared his throat. "That penis. Indicates she did more for him than cook dinner."

"Seems that way." Shields walked out of the room, calling from the landing, "Mrs Roosay. Number ninety-seven!" as though *he'd* been the one to get the tip and they'd known nothing about it until he'd just said.

Oliver stopped himself thinking like that, or being riled by Shields' arrogant ways. He wanted to find Glenn so those drugs were taken from her system and she was given some understanding somewhere. How old was she? If she was twelve or above, she'd be tried as an adult and sent away. He didn't think that was fair. She deserved help, a better life, a family who cared.

That she possibly wasn't going to get it had Oliver belting out of the room and down the stairs, back out onto the broken concrete path Glenn had trudged up and down all her life, leaving and entering a home where no one cared if she existed—except for the fact that she made cups of tea, cooked meals and gave her father more than he had a right to take.

Chapter Ten

Mrs Roosay turned out to be Mrs Rosé, a French woman of indeterminate years. She stood on her doorstep, back hunched, shoulders rounded, and squinted at them through thick-lensed glasses. Her home-knitted cardigan, brown with hints of beige running through it, crossed over at the front, her arms clamping the garment to her.

"Glenn, you say?"

"Yes, madam." Langham smiled. "Have you seen her today. Or recently?"

Oliver studied her. She didn't display body language that spoke of her withholding information. Or holding a child in her home. She looked weary, tired deep in her bones, and bewildered that a detective stood on her front path asking about a little girl.

"I have not seen her for weeks. I have been worried, but there is nothing I can do. The authorities, they do not listen to me. Say it is 'all in hand'. I do not believe them. How can it be all in hand if the child is still dirty and uncared for?"

Tears filled her eyes, and Oliver cursed the fact that here was a woman who had tried to help, yet her warm heart and good intentions had seemingly been brushed away.

"Did you allow Glenn into your home at any time, Mrs Rosé?" Langham's voice was soft, kind.

She nodded. "I would rather tell you inside. Please, come in."

Mrs Rosé led the way into her living room, the house the same layout as Glenn's. Except this home was clean and well cared for. Family photographs covered the walls and every available surface—end tables, the mantel, the television — and the air smelt of furniture polish and washing detergent. Glenn must have loved it here and wondered how her home could be so different.

Oliver and Langham sat at Mrs Rosé's gesture to do so, on an overstuffed sofa covered in pink chintz. She sat in a matching chair to their right and gazed out of the front window with rheumy eyes.

"She is a dear little thing. I waited for her. To come here and visit. But she did not come. The last time she was here was my birthday." She looked at Langham, her smile sad and watery.

"When was that, Mrs Rosé?" he asked.

"Two months ago. August seventeenth. She said she had made me a card, that she would bring it..." Her lower lip quivered.

"And the time before that?" Langham prodded.

"Every week on a Saturday morning. I have missed her. I wondered if the authorities had finally listened to me and taken her away because I saw her getting into someone's car. That car had been outside the house before, and the child had spoken to whoever was inside. Through the window."

She'd grabbed Oliver's attention with that.

Langham's too. The detective sat up straighter, then leant forward to take the old woman's hand in his. "Can you remember what day that was?"

She nodded. "A Friday. The Friday after she had been here on the Saturday." She frowned, as though the date eluded her. "I cannot remember..."

"I can work the date out, Mrs Rosé, don't worry about that." Langham gave her a gentle smile. "The car. Can you remember it?"

She nodded. "Very expensive. Black. With one of those badges on the front. A Mercedes. The man who collected her did not enter her house or knock on the door. I had been pruning in the front garden and saw Glenn pass. She did not see me. Her head was down, as usual. But she looked up just before she got to the car. The man got out and folded his arms on the roof just above his open door. He smiled, talked to her, but I cannot tell you what it was about. I could not hear. Glenn nodded, and he reached inside the car. He handed her something. Perhaps a cake, I am not sure, but she ate it there on the path."

Mrs Rosé raised one hand to her heart and closed her eyes. "Then the man walked around the front of the car and opened the passenger side. Glenn nodded, smiled up at him, and it seemed that she knew him because she got inside. Then he drove away and I have not seen her since." She stared at Langham. "I should have telephoned the police. But I thought... The car had been before..."

Langham patted her hand. "It's fine, Mrs Rosé. Please don't worry or blame yourself. You've been a great help. This may be a long shot, but did you happen to notice the licence plate?"

She smiled and pulled her hand from his. Stood on rickety legs and shivered over to the mantel. "Now *that* I can help you with. I had seen the car so often, but that was not the reason I remembered the plate. I wrote it down but have not forgotten it." She took a slip of paper from behind one of the photographs and handed it to Langham.

Oliver leaned across to read it. In her spidery handwriting, Mrs Rosé had given them shocking information. It was a personal plate. Just a name. One Oliver hadn't expected to see. It had to be a mistake. Was that man capable of abducting a child? It went against the grain, all he stood for—unless he'd turned into one of the bad guys recently. Oliver looked at Langham, who had paled significantly. It wasn't an uncommon name. Could belong to any number of men. And besides, there was no way a cop could afford a Mercedes. Not unless someone had died and left him shitloads of money.

5H13LD5.

He wasn't imagining it, was he? Wanting to see something that would bring that smarmy wanker down?

Langham cleared his throat. "Thank you, Mrs Rosé, you've been more help than you can imagine."

"Will you... Will you come back and tell me when you find her?" The old woman smoothed her skirt then patted her hair. "I have grown to love her. Would not wish ill on her."

"Of course," Langham said. "And if I don't call round, I'll telephone, all right?"

She nodded, then wrote down her phone number. After handing it to Langham, she showed them to the door on unsteady legs, fingers fluttering beside her.

They stepped outside, the front door closing behind them with a soft snick, and Oliver inhaled a deep breath. He had so many questions battering around inside his head he knew a headache wouldn't be long in coming. The lack of sleep was getting to him too—he was all liquid bones and weary muscles—but his brain, man, it buzzed. He walked to the end of the path, turning to see Langham still standing by the front door, finger and thumb toying with his lips as he stared at the carefully cut grass. It reminded Oliver of when the detective stared at the carpet, how he'd got so angry about it, then their resulting closeness.

Langham lowered his hand. "It can't be him, can it?" He looked up, frown firmly in place, mouth a hard laceration across his face. "I mean, he's a cop. So fucking righteous. So *correct* all the damn time."

"People change," Oliver said. "Who knows what the lure of money does. If he's involved, that is. If that's the way this is panning out."

Langham nodded, gaze back on the ground, although he walked towards Oliver and met him on the pavement. "You reckon he has it in him to be involved? To be on some psycho's payroll? Taking a kid, for fuck's sake?"

Oliver swallowed. "I'd like to say no. That the way he carries on tells us he's well into law enforcement, wouldn't be involved in anything dodgy. But honestly? He's a bastard—I've always said that. An out-and-out bastard.

With that personality? He's capable of anything, if you ask me."

Langham nodded again. "Shit. So what do we do? Ask him? Watch him? Tell the chief?"

"No idea, man. Not my call. Unless you're not asking me, just thinking out loud."

"Both. I'm stumped."

"There's a first time for everything."

Langham looked up.

Oliver smiled. "For what it's worth—my opinion, that is—I say we have him watched, see where he goes, what he does."

"Have him watched? That means letting someone else in on this. Trusting someone not to tell him."

"Right. Uh, right. What about running that plate. Should be the first thing you get done anyway—stupid of me to suggest anything else. Might not even be him. Just us jumping the gun. We'd look stupid approaching him without doing that first."

"Yep. Right. Come on."

Oliver trailed him down the street, back towards Glenn's home. Shields was outside, a posturing peacock, tail feathers splayed as though he'd caught some woman on his sexual radar. But no woman was around. He was alone, strutting up and down the path, mobile phone to his ear.

Langham held his arm out, stopping Oliver mid-stride. He tugged him closer to a hedge high enough to hide behind and not be seen. Close enough to hear. "Listen…"

"It's not like that," Shields said. "Well, that's what I'm about to do, go and find her. That's my job… No, I didn't expect for her to escape—no one did… Like I *meant* for this to happen? Muddy the waters? Christ, the last thing I want is my job complicated. Bad enough we had Alex going around killing people, let alone her."

Who was he speaking to? Not knowing burned Oliver up. It could be an innocent conversation, but that licence plate coming to light had shed a whole new slant on what

Shields was saying. He could be talking to Jackson...

Oliver remembered a time similar to this, back when he'd been a kid. The evidence in an overheard conversation had pointed to the speaker, his sister, being guilty of having sex, to being involved in something she shouldn't have been at fourteen years old, and he'd gone flat-out and accused her, told his parents too. Probably to divert attention from himself—he got too much of that with his 'weird ways'. Turned out she'd been discussing her homework, the latest gossip-fest about sex education the previous week. She'd been subjected to their mother marching her down to the doctors, having her checked out. Mum never could do anything by halves. Had to always have proof.

"Your ghosts tell you that?" his mum had said. "They tell you to get your sister into trouble?"

He'd shaken his head, tears welling, the flame of getting it wrong flaring in his gut. Bile had flashed up his windpipe, and he'd moved to walk away, unable to face her.

"Don't you bloody walk away from me, you little freak. You've got a lot to answer for. Always did act up, didn't you, wanting more attention." She'd planted meaty fists on equally meaty hips. "That's what this ghost shit is all about, isn't it? You getting attention. Well, it stops and stops now, you hear me?"

He'd nodded, prayed the voices would leave him alone, hurt on their behalf that they were getting the blame for this. They hadn't said a word, his sister had, and he'd read it wrong. Wrong, wrong, wrong!

Shame burned Oliver's cheeks now. He never wanted to feel that way again—the overwhelming guilt, sadness that he'd caused his sister such embarrassment. Even though it was that arsehole Shields in question now, Oliver still couldn't bring himself to accuse the man.

"It might be innocent," he whispered. "We might be hearing what we want to hear, having it sound like we want it to."

Langham gritted his teeth. "Shh."

Oliver strained to listen some more.

Shields coughed lightly, then, "Langham? He's interviewing a neighbour. What? Am I worried about that? Why should I be?"

Oliver's guts bunched. *Innocent conversation? Is whoever is on the other end of that line reminding him his car might have been clocked in this street? Berating him on that personal plate?*

Shields laughed, strutted up and down some more. "Hell, no. I'll give Mrs Roosay a visit once Langham's gone. Check what he said to her. Whether she saw anything."

Panic thudded through Oliver. That had sounded sinister, like Shields would be warning Mrs Rosé off. He struggled to work out whether these were just his thoughts or if the spirits were whispering to him, telling him what Shields had in mind. Confused as to what to believe, he closed his eyes, tried to tune in to the other side, begging for someone to come through.

Nothing. No one.

"Right," Shields said. "Damn right. We'll have this one dealt with in no time."

Oliver couldn't stand it any longer. He snapped his eyes open and walked forward, out into the open, making his way towards Shields. The detective had his back to him, his greasy hair shining despite the pale, feeble sunlight. On Glenn's path, a crisp packet crinkled under Oliver's tread.

Shields spun around, eyes narrowed, his eyebrows quivering. "Yes, I hear you, sir. Will do." He snapped his phone closed, stared harder at Oliver. "Where's Langham?"

"Here," Langham said, his voice gruff, barely concealed emotion sneakily bristling out of him. He looked as though he struggled to keep himself in control, that those emotions showing themselves could fuck right off and not come back. Like he didn't need the display giving him away.

"Any news from the Roosay woman?"

"No," Langham said quickly. Too quickly. "She's just some old French woman." He shrugged and shook his head. "So now we need to regroup, work out what we've done so far, who's dealing with what and where we go from here."

Was it Oliver's imagination, or did Shields sigh with relief just then?

"Right." Shields whipped out a notebook. "Go for it."

Langham acted cool, his emotions back in check. "Louise is at the morgue, her scene still being searched. Mark Reynolds, I presume, is in the same place, his scene being inspected. The old woman, Reynolds' grandmother. What's the status on that?"

"She's with Louise and Mark." Shields jotted in his pad.

"And Ronan Dougherty?"

"Last I heard he was still in situ."

Oliver studied Shields while the man's head was bent. He looked for signs of discomfort, of guilt, but found none. Either he was one clever bastard at disguising how he felt, at acting innocent, or he had nothing to do with this. Not knowing for sure would eat away at Oliver, his past accusation leaving him indecisive, unsure of what to believe.

"And then there's these two." Langham wrote in his own pad. "Three, including the foetus. You dealing with them?"

He'll say yes, because then he can visit Mrs Rosé. Can't see him taking Langham's word for it that the old bird doesn't know anything. Shit.

"May as well, seeing as I was first on the scene." He smirked, like Langham being out of the loop at that house in the middle of nowhere had made him a lesser detective. "I'll also put things in motion to find Glenn." He chuckled. "Glenn Close. Jesus..."

Arsehole.

"Fine," Langham said. "The men at the house are being dealt with—must get an update on how that's going. Any news on Jackson?"

"He's being watched until the warrant comes through to search Privo," Shields said.

The man looked affronted, as if Langham questioning him wasn't right. As if having to answer to him didn't sit well. Of course, it wouldn't, Shields being Shields, but Oliver looked at him with new eyes now. Wanted to find the buried nugget that proved he was in on this shit. He shook his head, thinking of the times Shields had accused him of having a hand in the murders Oliver had brought to their attention, when all along he was — *possibly* — involved in shit like that himself.

"So we're up to date. I'll call in, see if there are any tox results back yet. Yep, I've got high hopes on that, but I want to know what the hell's in those sugar strands that makes a person act like this." Langham gestured to the house, arm raised, then let it slap back down to his side. "This has turned into a fucking nightmare."

Shields turned away, muttered, "And it'll only get worse."

"What was that?" Langham said.

Oliver's instincts screamed that Shields was guilty, but he shushed the roaming thoughts — the words sliding through his mind sounded too much like his own voice, not those of the dead. He couldn't trust it, just couldn't.

"Let's pray it doesn't get worse," Shields said, louder this time, before disappearing inside the house, that damn hanky covering his nose and mouth.

That's not what you said the first time. Not what you fucking said!

"Come on." Langham strode towards his car, stiff limbed, anger seeping out of him. He raked a hand through his hair, tightened it into a fist and jerked open the driver's-side door with a more-than-annoyed tug.

Oliver trotted to keep up then climbed inside the car, knowing exactly what he was about to hear. Or was that what he *hoped* to hear? Shit, he wasn't sure — wasn't sure of anything anymore. He needed sleep, a clear head for this crap. To see things objectively and not as a jumble of suspicious words.

Langham started the car. "If it isn't him, if he isn't involved, I'll eat my fucking badge." He let the engine idle, taking his phone out of his inside jacket pocket. Stared at

Mrs Rosé's phone number. Jabbed his phone buttons. "Mrs Rosé? Ah, hello again. It's Detective Langham. I was at your house a short while ago. No, we haven't found her. I'm calling on another matter." He glanced at Oliver, his face grim. "If another detective calls at your door, don't answer. In fact, if anyone you don't know knocks, ignore them. For now. Until I get back to you. Why? It's better that you deal with me, seeing as I spoke with you. That all right? I'll send someone out to keep an eye on you." He waited a beat, then said goodbye, dropping his phone back into his pocket. "That's her safe and sorted. Now, I think we need to visit Ronan Dougherty's place, see him for ourselves, unless he's been moved since Shields last got an update." He clamped the steering wheel. "Fuck. The licence plate. Must remember to run that through the computer."

Chapter Eleven

Ronan Dougherty looked disgusting. No other word for it. Not only had his arms been hacked off, but he'd been eviscerated, his insides outside, much like Glenn's mother. They sat in a pile on his stomach, the skin of which was pulled back like a half-peeled orange, forgotten by the person who had wanted to eat it. Blood coated the beige carpet beneath him, a living room carpet that, everywhere else, was clean and well cared for. Ronan's place was tidy — a man who liked order, cleanliness, Oliver guessed — the surfaces recently polished, now marred by arcs of blood splatter that spoke of a frenzied knife attack. The way the blood had landed on the walls and ceiling indicated it had been cast off, droplets flying off a knife before the blade was plunged back into the body.

Alex had been angry here, unable to contain it. Had stabbed and stabbed, possibly long after Ronan had died. Those drugs, God, they changed a human into a monster.

Langham sighed, standing on one leg to put on a protective bootie. "I've seen angry kills before, but this is something else. Think of Louise. Imagine what she'd have looked like if you hadn't turned up. Yep, Alex went back, finished what he'd started, but her body wasn't like this one. This resembles Glenn's parents. It's like they killed her together — but we know they didn't."

"Maybe they escalate with each kill." Oliver cocked his head, waiting for Ronan to make contact. He wasn't sure if he could take that now, if he could listen to what the poor man had to say. He was tired. So fucking tired. "Maybe the drugs make them worse the longer they take them. Higher doses or whatever. Could produce differing results from the same killer."

Bootied up, Langham stepped forward, then crouched beside the body. "The strands are here. Most definitely Alex's work."

Oliver stepped from foot to foot, his booties rustling. No way was he getting any closer to that body. Like Louise the second time around, Ronan had no face. His scalp had been treated like an orange too, yanked back to expose a bloody, rounded dome of skull with a harsh, jagged divot marring it.

"Blunt force trauma," Langham said. "Looks like the butt of a gun. Rectangular."

"But if Alex had a gun and just wanted to kill to stop Ronan speaking out, why not just shoot him?"

"Because the drugs make him want to kill in a frenzy, to obliterate the victim bearing any resemblance to a human being. I'm guessing, by the way, but that makes sense to me. Feels like I'm on the right track. If you just want to kill someone, to keep their mouth shut, you generally don't see this kind of rage. Rage means emotion, a connection, that it's personal."

"So Alex took it personally that Louise and Ronan had made moves to expose him, the Privo shit, is that it?"

"Who knows?" Langham stood, stared down at the body. "He was messed up well before the drugs by the sound of it. Those strands, his grandmother — can't have been a healthy upbringing, *if* he's to be believed. The old dear might not have done any of it, like Mark said."

Oliver thought about the similarities between himself, Alex and Glenn. He could so easily have been them. Mean parents, being taunted all his life, not fitting in anywhere. But he hadn't turned out bad, and who knew, maybe Alex and Glenn wouldn't have if they hadn't been force-fed drugs. Force-fed. Sounded more like they'd taken them willingly, so he couldn't even blame that on whoever had given the strands to them.

Of course they'd have taken them fucking willingly. Who wouldn't mind eating a doughnut like that if one was offered? Who'd suspect the strands on top would contain something that would change their lives forever?

Not Oliver. He'd have accepted it like he'd accept a biscuit with his cup of tea. Not Alex, who may well have been given one when he'd gone to blackmail Jackson. And not Glenn, who'd been probably so starved of not only love but confections, that she'd gobbled it down eagerly.

Like Langham had said, this was a fucking nightmare.

The coroner's men loitered, waiting for Langham's nod before they went about their business, removing the body and taking it to a place where the secrets hidden from the casual observer would be revealed. The morticians had one hell of a job on their hands today, the amount of bodies turning up in the state they were. Murders weren't unheard of here, but the volume, all at one time, was.

Oliver moved out of the way, standing close to the wall beside the door as Ronan's body was taken out, prone on a stretcher, the sight of him covered by a black bag from any prying eyes that might glance his way out there on the street.

What a shitty way to die.

"It is, isn't it?"

Oliver tensed. "Is that you?" He flapped one hand at Langham.

"Me? Yes, this is me." The man chortled. *"Didn't expect to see myself being carried out like that, but there you go. Life's full of surprises."*

Oliver smiled at Ronan's upbeat tone. "You sound all right about it."

"Well, there's nothing I can bloody do about it now, is there? No point pissing and moaning about something I can't change. May as well get on with my lot and be done with it."

"Good way of dealing with it, I s'pose. So, you have something you want to tell me?"

"Damn right I do. That's what I'm here for, isn't it, a bit of

gossip and all that?"

Oliver knew he'd have liked Ronan in life. "What can you tell me? What do you remember?"

"Well, after I started sticking my nose in where it clearly wasn't wanted" —another chuckle— *"I found out something a bit surprising. I mean, it all points to it being Jackson, doesn't it? I thought the same, but the man hasn't got any fucking idea what's going on right under his nose."*

Oliver frowned. "But that doesn't make sense. After we visited Privo—"

"Yep, I know. I kinda tagged along for the ride there. He was getting rid of some other stuff. Been making drugs for a rival company, hasn't he, the dirty bastard. He doesn't own Privo, just runs the place. The owner leaves it to him, no questions asked, just rakes in the cash, thanks very much."

"So he was removing other drugs? Totally unrelated to the strands?"

"Yup. Shitting himself, he is. Funny to watch. Anyway, the owner would be a bit pissed off about Jackson making money on the side, so Jackson's covering his arse by removing them."

"So does the owner have anything to do with the strands and what's going on there?"

"Fuck, yes. She's in on it."

"She?"

"Yep, and you wouldn't think it to look at her either. Not mentioning any names and all that, but some of us who've spoken to you haven't been telling the truth. Put it this way, they haven't lied, they just haven't told you everything. Maybe they're in denial, who knows?"

Oliver thought on who'd contacted him. Louise. Glenn's mother. Mark Reynolds. "Who?"

"Ah, I wouldn't like to say. It'd take the fun out of your investigation, wouldn't it?"

"But by you not saying, you're hampering it."

"So what do the police do when they don't have someone like you, who has someone like me filtering them information? They investigate, that's what."

Ronan's voice began to fade.

"Come on now, Ronan. That isn't fair. This isn't a game. You can't leave it hanging like this. Just give me a name. I can't contact spirits—they have to contact me—so it's not like I can burst into their death sleep or whatever and demand answers."

"Louise."

It came softly, a whisper of sound Oliver barely caught.

"You need to look into Louise."

"Into? As in, literally?"

Ronan didn't answer. His presence had gone, leaving Oliver battling a wave of fatigue.

"What did you get?" Langham asked, his face full of concern.

"Give me a second." Oliver held up his hand. "I'm knackered." He shook his head, willing some life back into his aching limbs. His broken finger throbbed so hard he had the urge to yank it off.

"Come on, into the car."

Oliver followed Langham outside, leaving the other detectives to it. Inside the vehicle, Oliver rested his head on the seat, eyes closing. It felt like he hadn't slept in days, like the first call from Louise had been months ago. He berated himself for not asking Ronan about Shields, but the conversation had taken on a life of its own.

Langham drove away, and Oliver kept his eyes closed until the car stopped again. He looked around, seeing nothing but a dingy street, the side walls of aged houses either side, the bricks uneven, knobbles and gouges spoiling them. Langham had parked, sandwiching the car between two others, and with no pedestrians in sight, it felt as though they were the only people on the planet.

"Talk to me." Langham leaned across, placed his hand on Oliver's thigh.

A shiver of…*something* snaked through Oliver. The contact was intimate yet bordered on friendly. Nothing to write home about. So why did his body hum the way it did? Stupid to ask himself that, really. He knew why.

"That was Ronan."

"I gathered that. And?"

Oliver turned his head, looked at Langham. Saw the crags from the detective being tired, the wrinkles beside his eyes that appeared deeper, more pronounced. Was that a smattering of grey at his temples too? Where had those hairs come from? "He said someone else lied to me. That we had to look into Louise. Whether he means inside her body or look into her life, I don't know."

"Louise? Did she give you the impression she was lying?"

"No, she sounded genuine enough, but now I think about it, she was hesitant. And she didn't give the right information. Remember? We thought she'd worked at Privo. She implied that. And she mentioned a 'she'. Wasn't too happy about her son being with her mother if I recall correctly."

"Family feuds happen all the time." Langham squeezed Oliver's thigh. Lightly.

"So what d'you reckon Ronan meant?" Oliver sighed out the words.

"She's probably got something on her, some evidence, something that will help us. If being dead is like I imagine it to be, you can float about all over the damn place and find out information. He's probably done that. Whatever, it all helps – any information helps."

"We still need to find out about those eyes, why they glow like that."

Langham stared at him, as though he thought of nothing but Oliver. That the case and all it entailed didn't swim around his brain. "There's a lot we need to do. Detectives all over the place, all dealing with different victims. What started out as a case between me and Shields has expanded. Possibly too many chefs in the kitchen, but what can we do?"

Oliver didn't know. "And shit, I forgot to say. Jackson isn't in on it."

Langham frowned. "You're kidding me. That man looked guilty as fucking sin."

"He *is* guilty, but not of drugging Alex and those kids. He's working for the competition, using Privo as a place to mass produce drugs for them. That was what he was getting rid of."

"Fuck me. If we'd known that before… What a waste of time and resources. Gimme a sec." He grabbed the radio, asking for, then being connected to the detective dealing with the Jackson side of things. "Yeah, you got Jackson at the station now? Okay, is he talking? Ah, right. A lot of denial. That's because he doesn't know what the fuck you're talking about. Ask him questions leading to an answer on whether he's making a quick quid on the side. See if he grabs the chance to admit to that—it's gotta be better for him than taking the blame for this other shit. Yeah, right. That's what I thought." He relayed what Oliver had told him. "Okay? So go with that. Thanks."

"A massive can of worms." Oliver watched the tic flickering beneath Langham's eye. Wanted to kiss it to make it stop.

"It is. I need my bed."

Could Oliver be bothered to give one of his usual retorts? No, he couldn't. He needed his bed, too, more than he ever had before. Speaking to so many dead people in one day had taken its toll. Zapped the energy out of him. He could just close his eyes now, sleep forever, using Langham's crotch as a pillow.

"Too much to do, though," Oliver slurred, giving in and allowing his eyes to shut.

"Yep. We need to run that Mercedes plate. Need to find out who owns Privo. Need to deal with Louise." Langham sounded as weary as Oliver felt. His voice was closer, his breath hot on Oliver's cheek. "Need to make good our date."

Langham's tongue did *not* just dart out and taste Oliver's lips then. Did it?

The wetness on Oliver's mouth proved it. He licked his lips, keeping his eyes closed, and waited to see what Langham would do next. It only took a smidgen of time before the detective pressed his mouth to his. Oliver, shocked yet insanely pleased, responded by opening up. His first kiss with the detective was better than he'd imagined it would be, all soft, probing tongues and heated breaths. Wandering hands, touching so lightly it was like they barely touched at all. Tiny groans from the pair of them, intermingling to become one. Fuck, this was hot, something he'd wanted for too long now. It was just a shame they were bang in the middle of a case, sitting in a car in a street where anyone could peer inside the car should they have a mind. Hardly the time and place to be indulging in carnal pleasures, but Oliver was damned if he could pull away, to stop the kiss that made his cock throb, his balls tighten and his nipples harden.

Langham's mouth left his, and he peppered kisses across Oliver's cheek to his earlobe. He sucked the plump softness inside, swirling his tongue, sending Oliver to a place he'd previously only visited in his daydreams, his dreams at night. A hoarse groan escaped Oliver, one he hadn't expected to erupt, and it startled his eyes open. Langham appraised him as he kissed and sucked, and the knowledge of that turned Oliver on to such a degree that pre-cum oozed from his dick.

"Jesus, Langham," he breathed, chest as tight as his balls. "We can't... D'you *like* picking places where we can't go on? Where we might get caught?"

He released Oliver's earlobe. "No, it just happens that way. I wish we were at your place, my place, anywhere but here."

"Me too, but we have to go. Too much to get done." He panted as Langham moved his hand up Oliver's thigh to cover his bulging erection. The touch almost sent Oliver over the edge. "And it isn't...like I don't want us to do this. Me...saying we ought to get going. But we...do."

111

Langham kneaded, tongue flashing across Oliver's lower lip.

"Fuck, Langham, will you *stop* that? We'll get caught!"

Langham pulled away, leaving a void in his wake. Oliver wanted that hand back on his cock, that tongue back in his mouth.

"So," Langham said, all business again. "After we run the plate at the station and find out who owns Privo, we go to the morgue."

Oliver woke right up out of his sexual stupor over that. He sat upright, mouth agape for a few seconds. Then, "What?"

"You heard me. The morgue. You need to get your feet wet there sometime. Besides, we've still got our booties on. May as well put them to good use."

Oliver stared down at his feet. "They're dirty. We'll need clean ones."

"Whatever. Excuses won't work. We need to see Louise. And you wanted it this way, remember? Wanted in on everything this time."

Oliver had—did—but the thought of seeing Louise in such a sterile place, tools poking into places they had no right to be, made his guts roll over. "Right. Yeah."

He remained silent as Langham drove them back to the station, his mind not on Louise and what lay ahead, but on what had just happened. They'd kissed. They'd fucking kissed! Jesus Christ, he wanted to smile so hard that his cheeks hurt. Wanted to punch the air and let out a childish whoop. But he didn't. Instead, he kept quiet, reliving the feel of his man's tongue on his, the way it had probed, investigating the contours of his mouth for the first time, Oliver reciprocating. It had felt good, all kinds of right, and he couldn't wait for the next phase.

But he'd have to. The station appeared out of nowhere as Oliver came out of his daydream, the car parked, engine shut off. They exited, strode inside the station as though what had occurred between them hadn't, and went into Langham's office. The detective sat at his desk, tapping the keys and moving the mouse. He threw himself back into his chair with a sigh, the chair scooting backwards a bit, banging into a metal filing cabinet behind.

"It isn't him," he said. "Yet I could have sworn it was."

Was it weird for Oliver to feel relief? "Who is it, then?"

"A woman. Cordelia Shields. Fifty-four. Lives in that big house up by the river. You know the one?"

Yeah, Oliver knew it. Reminded him of a damn mansion every time he saw it, with those white walls and fake Greek columns holding up a veranda that skirted halfway up the property and all around. He'd often wondered who lived there, and now he knew, although the name didn't ring any bells.

"So now we need to know why a man was driving her car, why he visited Glenn and why the fuck he took her away."

Oliver nodded. The day was pushing into evening, which meant time was pressing if they wanted to visit Louise then Cordelia Shields. And if they wanted to quit work, have their date, and get some damn sleep.

"Morgue first?" Oliver asked.

"Yeah, morgue first. I'm beginning to think this fucking day will never end."

"Me too."

Chapter Twelve

The overhead morgue lights gleamed onto the metal table holding Louise's remains, the glare bright enough to hurt Oliver's eyes. To actually be here, with different scents combating for dominance—the tart stench of disinfectant, the whiff of dead bodies, his fresh sweat—gave him a sense of disembodiment. Like he viewed it on a screen, wasn't *really* here with a room along the corridor holding drawer upon drawer of corpses. Who the fuck would *choose* this as a profession? Who would want those smells inside their noses even after they went home? Those smells seeping deep into their skin so they were never free of them despite bathing? He felt dirty, wanted a shower so badly, so God knew what the mortician felt like. Maybe he was used to it. Maybe even *liked* it.

Oliver wanted to throw up at the thought.

But that mortician, a kind-eyed, black-haired, rotund man of about forty, tended to Louise with such care and respect that Oliver changed his mind about him and his job. Someone had to do it.

Langham introduced the man to Oliver as Hank, and Oliver would have shaken his hand in any other circumstance, but the bloodied latex gloves ensured he kept his arms by his sides.

"I've sent the sugar strands and some hairs—fortunately for us some have the root still attached—to forensics. Other hairs, well, they're not real. I'd say they were synthetic," Hank said.

Langham nodded, stepped closer to the table. "Yes, the guy wore a wig. We know who he is anyway, but the confirmation would only strengthen our case."

"Ah, always the last to know these things, me." Hank smiled and continued his perusal of Louise's insides. "Nasty business, this. And there's more of them there, waiting in their silent way for me to find out what they have to say despite being dead." He nodded over at three more tables, bodies covered with white sheets.

Oliver wondered why they weren't refrigerated while Hank worked on Louise, but he dreaded the answer he'd receive. There might not be enough room in the fridges… Best to mind his own business.

"All related murders, I'm told," Hank went on. He walked to a shiny whiteboard on the wall beside the door. "A Mark Reynolds, Geraldine Reynolds and Ronan Dougherty here as well as Louise. I really ought to get them in the fridge, but I'm short-handed today." He eyed them with hope. "No? Don't fancy helping me cart them down the way? Didn't think you would. So, this is a serial, yes?" He moved back over to Louise, peeling back what was left of the skin on her face.

Oliver felt like fainting.

"Serial, yes," Langham said. "You'll have more bodies in shortly. Male and female. Although they're related in the case to these poor bastards, they weren't killed by the same person. If you'll believe it, a young girl killed them."

Hank shot his head up, stared at Langham with his mouth wide open. "What, a young girl killed these people here?"

"No, a man killed these four, but the girl killed the two you've got coming in. When you see the female victim, you'll wonder how a four-foot kid had the strength to do what she did, but she had the help of drugs."

"Oh my. Well…" Hank picked up an electric blade. "That sounds most disturbing. Youth of today, eh? Any road, is there anything I can help you with, because I need to…you know. Off with her head!" He slashed at the air with his blade, his red cheeks shining with sweat.

Oliver's knees buckled, and he grabbed the table behind

him, shrieking at having touched a sheet-covered foot.

Hank laughed. "Not literally, dear boy. Just cutting the top off. Need to have a wee look at her brain."

Bile surged up Oliver's throat and settled on the back of his tongue. Good job he hadn't eaten lately, otherwise what he'd consumed would have splattered all over the floor. He had to get the hell out of here.

"We just needed to take a look inside Louise here, unless you can tell us what we need to know. Not that we even know what we're looking for," Langham said. "Inside her torso. Did you find anything there other than the strands and the hairs?"

"A bit of fibre, nothing to tell the neighbours about," Hank said. "Apart from the fact she was hacked more after death than when she was alive, and she received an almighty whack to the back of the head with a rounded object — think metal piping, something like that — there's nothing to report here. The others?" He shrugged. "Won't know until I open them up, and that's just a saying. They're pretty much opened up already, except for the old lady. Kind killer, thinking of me like that, saving me a job." He smiled, laughed again then gave his blade a burst of electricity. "Sorry I couldn't be more help."

"If you find anything—"

"I'll let you know. Chop-chop!" He brought the blade humming to life again and pulled a transparent visor off a table towards him. He held it up. "Wouldn't mind putting that on for me, would you? My hands are a bit messy."

As Langham stepped around the table to give his services, Oliver bolted from the room. How could Hank be so *jolly*? If Oliver had that job, he'd be as morose as hell. He leaned against the wall in the corridor, the sinister sound of the blade rasping on his nerves, and closed his eyes. He wanted to be sick, to run and to sleep all at the same time. Do anything to make this shit go away. Now he realised why he should have just left it at Louise's murder site, gone home after giving a statement and forgot the whole thing.

Let Langham do his job alone. And how did *he* manage to keep it all together with a job like that? His admiration for the detective grew.

Langham came out of the room, leaned one hand against the wall over Oliver's head and looked at him with concern. "You okay?"

"I will be when we get out of here." Oliver breathed in deeply, tasting death.

"Yep, we're going right now. I don't know what's up with me today, but I forgot to run a check on who owns Privo. I'll call it in to Shields, let him deal with it. I want to visit Cordelia Shields before it gets too late. Then we're calling it a day. Everything will still be here tomorrow when we wake up, still one massive fucking mess."

It was with huge relief that Oliver stepped outside into the fresh air, although faint traces of odours still lived inside his nose. He briefly wondered how long it would take for them to go away, then dismissed the thought when his stomach rumbled. How could he eat after being in there? All right, he'd seen Louise's body in that field, but it had been different somehow. That sterile room had brought it home, really brought it home, that she was dead. What had he thought before, then? That she was a parody of a dead body lying in the grass? He didn't know — his thoughts a jumble, coming at him from all directions until his head spun. He lurched forward, hands out to brace his fall, but Langham caught hold of his arm.

"You all right?" he asked.

"Uh, yeah. No. I need food. Sleep."

"You and me both. Oh, and welcome to my world."

"You can keep it." Oliver walked towards Langham's car, the detective still gripping his arm. "I don't know how you do this day in, day out."

At the car, Langham saw Oliver seated inside before he answered. He leaned into the open doorway, one hand on top of the car, the other dangling beside him. "It isn't like this all the time, you know. This shit is a one-off."

"Yeah, well. Rather you than me on a full-time basis."

"Listen." He brought his hand up to stroke Oliver's face. "We'll visit this Shields woman, and then I swear to you we're going to your place, my place, or some fucking place, all right?"

Oliver nodded. "All right."

* * * *

Seeing the house by the river from this distance wasn't something Oliver had thought he'd ever do. Looking at it from afar and wondering who lived inside was as close as he'd thought he would ever get. Now, standing on the semicircular, red-brick front step beneath the veranda, his stomach rumbling and churning, he imagined what Cordelia Shields would look like.

The door swung open before the reverberating sound of the bell had died.

Cordelia Shields' face was that of someone so much younger than fifty-four. Surgery had been kind to her, smoothing out the wrinkles she would undoubtedly have had, had she not gone under the knife. Blonde hair, salon perfect, graced her head in copious waves, some coiling on her shoulders only to continue their tumble down her chest. The ends reached below her breasts—large, augmented breasts. She sported the body of a twenty-something, well-toned and lithe. Her jogging bottoms clung to slim legs, to hips Oliver might have admired if he were that way inclined.

He glanced at Langham quickly, but if the detective were aware he didn't show it. He kept his gaze on Mrs Shields.

"Sorry to trouble you, madam." Langham drew out his badge. "Detective Langham. Would you mind talking to us about your car?"

"My car?" She frowned and brought one hand up to rest on her throat, the hand the only part of her that gave away her age. It was craggy with wrinkles. "Which *one*, darling?"

Her laugh got on Oliver's nerves.

"Your black Mercedes with the licence plate 5-H-1-3-L-D-5."

"What about it?" She smirked and arched one eyebrow, cocked her hip, leaned it against the door jamb.

Langham cleared his throat. "Who else drives it but you?"

"I don't *drive* it." She waved a hand in a dismissive manner, pristine, long, red-polished fingernails catching a strand of her hair. "Although someone drives me *around* in it."

Ah, it was like that, was it? Definitely one of those people.

"When was the last time it was used?" Langham asked, his voice compact.

Oliver wondered if they were going to talk about this on the doorstep all night or whether this rude woman would actually invite them in. He was dying to sit down, even if only for five minutes. His head ached, his broken finger ached—hell, his whole damn body ached.

"This morning. Robert took me into the city." She smiled tightly.

"Robert?"

"My driver."

"And the time before that?"

"Hmmm, let me think. Perhaps it was yesterday. Did I go out yesterday? Hmm, I'm not sure. I'll have to consult my diary. Wait here one moment."

She disappeared inside and closed the door before Langham could stop her.

"Shit. She could be doing anything in there. Warning this Robert." Langham grimaced and ran a palm over his now-stubbled chin.

"You have a suspicious mind," Oliver said.

"I have every reason to. Especially as her car is involved in an abduction."

"Point taken."

They stood on that red step, statues of impatience as they waited an interminably long time for Mrs Shields to return.

"What the fuck is she *doing* in there?" Langham muttered, the tic working beneath his eye again.

He was tired, that much was certain, and Oliver selfishly wondered if the detective would be too tired for their date. "This house is so big, she might have to walk a fair way to wherever she keeps her diary."

"Ridiculous having a house this big," Langham said. "Probably only her and a husband, a few hired help. What's the point? Why not downsize?"

Oliver disagreed. "Why *not* have it if she can? Why does she need to live in a smaller house if she can afford to live here?"

Langham looked at him as though he'd grown horns. "You serious? This place should be filled with people, not one or two rattling around, voices echoing."

"It might have been, once. She might have had several kids, they've left the nest, and now there's just her and possibly her old man left. It's still her home. She shouldn't have to leave it, leave all the memories behind because other people think the place is too big for her."

"Other people. You mean me. Just say it."

"Yep, you. Entitled to your opinion and all that, but I don't see it the same way."

"Didn't ask you to."

"Nope, you didn't." Oliver stopped it there. He wasn't in the mood for their sniping, and the tone Langham had used meant it would be more than banter if they continued this way. "So, what happens if she comes back saying she never went out yesterday or any of the days that car was spotted at Glenn's?"

Langham didn't respond. The front door swung open on well-oiled hinges, and Mrs Shields stood there again, diary in hand.

"Well, I didn't go out yesterday. I thought I had, but after looking in here I see I have my days mixed up."

Old age crept up on you even if your body looked younger.

"Does...Robert use the car for his own purposes?"

Langham cocked his head.

"No, he most certainly does not!" Indignation came off her like sleet—pointed and sharp, stinging and cold. "He lives in—I would know if he used it without my permission. Why ever would you ask such a thing?"

"May we come in, Mrs Shields?"

Oliver watched for her reaction. He felt she was hiding something, although he couldn't get a handle on exactly what it was.

"Is that necessary?" She pursed her mouth, agitation making her top lip gain a row of vertical lines much like comb teeth.

"It would be more comfortable..." Langham sniffed, smiled.

"I would *much* rather we spoke out here." She glanced back into the house, a large foyer with gleaming white tiles and a mahogany staircase at the centre, shooting straight up to a veranda much like the one outside the house. Gaze back on them, eyes wider, though she hid any anxiety very well, she said, "Just tell me what the problem is and I will deal with it. Broken back light? Did I forget to purchase new road tax? Flat tyre? What?"

Oliver wanted to laugh. She was good at this acting innocent business.

"None of those, madam." Langham sighed, his irritation with her game obvious.

"Then what, for God's sake?" She clamped her lips closed, sucking them in so their rose hue disappeared.

They reminded Oliver of a shaved vagina.

Jesus. I need sleep...

His man coughed. "How about child abduction?"

Her mouth sagged open. Colour, pink as a tongue, formed rounded spots on her cheekbones. A gasp came out of her, asphyxiated, torn, an after-thought—that gasp should have come first, shouldn't it? "Child abduction? Whatever do you *mean?*"

"Exactly what I said, madam."

"Surely not!" She moved back a few inches, started closing the door. "There is no way my baby would be involved in such a thing."

"Your baby? Would that be Robert?"

She rolled her eyes, the irises disappearing for a moment, her whites blood-veined, bulging. "No! My baby! My *car!*"

"Right, Mrs Shields. I'll be frank with you. I'm tired. Very tired. I'm investigating several murders. A child is missing, taken by a man driving your *baby*. Now, either you let me in, or I call for back-up." Langham glanced about. "Your neighbours…they're close enough to see your driveway. See a few patrol cars travelling up it. Is that what you want?" He shrugged. "With my car, us two standing here, we could be salesmen. Do you understand what I'm saying?"

He said that last statement like he spoke to a dense child. Yeah, he was tired — overtired.

She blinked several times. "I really don't think —"

"I don't care what you think. I am coming into your house to ask questions whether you want me to or not. Whether it's now or later, I don't care. Unless you prefer to accompany me down to the station. Would that suit you better? Of course, we would drive you, not Robert. Your car. It will have to be collected. Forensics will need to check it."

"I am telling you, Detective, my baby wouldn't transport an abducted child."

She spoke as though her car was a living being. Was she cracked in the fucking head? Oliver was starting to lose patience with her as well. He had the urge to shove her into the damn house, march her to a sofa and get some bloody answers.

"Your baby would have had no choice, because Robert, or a man at any rate, would have been *driving it!*" Langham snapped. "Where is Robert now?"

"I… I… He *was* here, but —"

"Convenient." Langham clenched his jaw, ground his teeth together so the muscles in his cheeks danced. "Listen,

I'm not into pussyfooting around you now. I'm going to call for another officer. He will bring uniformed officers with him, who will have your car towed away. You will speak to me and my colleague here, about the times Robert has driven your car with your knowledge. If you are so sure it hasn't been used without you in it, then you must have been present when he visited the home—several times, I might add—of the abducted girl before finally taking her away for good. Now, that girl was taken but has been able to get away from her abductors because she has *returned home and killed her parents today*." Langham bunched his fists. "We do not know where she is now, but I intend to find out. Your car was used to take her, so it isn't a far-fetched assumption that the young girl has been kept here. I have probable cause to enter this house without a warrant. Do. You. Understand. Mrs. Shields?"

"Yes. Yes! I'm not stupid!" She glanced back again.

What was she *doing*? Checking the coast was clear before she let them in? Stalling them? Oliver glanced at Langham, who opened his phone and walked back down the drive— the only way anyone could get off the property, unless they chose to dive into the river at the rear. He barked orders, striding across the gravel, his shoes crunching—Rice Krispies in milk, amplified—his face rigid. He finished his call, features now composed, flat and expressionless.

"Mrs Shields. You're married, correct?" he asked.

"Yes." Her hand fluttered at her throat again. "But only in name. He… We're separated. Have been for quite some time." She blustered on, "I…I was building up my career. He didn't like it. He… I earned more than him. We—"

"Your husband is a police officer. A detective?"

Oliver's guts twisted. *Jesus Christ…*

"Yes." She looked back again, damn her, cheeks redder now.

"A detective currently unavailable, one on duty, who, for reasons unknown, hasn't reported in and isn't answering his phone."

Oh, fuck me…

"What has that got to do with me where he goes?" She bit her bottom lip, the flesh around her two front teeth bleaching white.

"And you are the owner of PrivoLabs, correct?"

"Yes. And what of *that*?"

"Mrs Shields, I would like to take you into the city for questioning."

"I'm under arrest?" She let her jaw drop, a pathetic attempt to look dismayed, and shook her head.

"Not yet, no. But I have a feeling you will be."

Chapter Thirteen

Officers had arrived within minutes, oozing over the house and grounds like ants on a mission. Mrs Shields had been taken into the city, bristling and prickly as she'd been led to a police car. Oliver thought Langham's touch of having her escorted in a marked car amusing – if she was involved in this crap, she deserved to be seen, to have people know she was a criminal. A small part of him wondered whether that woman *could* be involved. She didn't look wily, didn't even seem the kind of woman who could head a huge corporation like that. There was no authority about her, really, only an indignant, belligerent air that most people he knew with money possessed.

And what about Shields himself? He was *married* to her? Christ, he hadn't said a damn word about that. He should have, what with PrivoLabs being involved. He shouldn't have even been a part of the case. How had he expected to keep that quiet? It would have come to light sooner or later. And did that mean he *was* involved in the abduction, in PrivoLabs' wrongdoings? Did he remain silent about everything so he was in on the ground floor, able to know where the investigation was going so he could warn Cordelia Shields? Was their separation a ruse?

Oliver didn't know, didn't fucking *know*, and as he followed Langham through the massive house, mind swimming with too many questions, he wasn't sure he *wanted* to know. Yeah, Shields taking a big fall was something he'd take pleasure in, he could admit that all right, but the way Shields had treated him, accusing *him* of being a killer all those times, when all along he'd been involved in something like this?

"Fucking stinks," he said, realising too late he'd spoken and not thought.

"Yep," Langham said. "Like a bacteria-riddled turd."

They were upstairs, wending in and out of the many bedrooms, finding no Glenn Close and nothing to imply she'd been there. Frustration burst from Langham, great bubbles of it with every sigh he gave, every grunt he made. Oliver wanted to pop them all, make them go away, but Langham was in detective mode and wouldn't rest until he got some answers.

"You getting anything?" Langham asked. "Any pushes from dead people?"

Oliver hadn't been taking any notice. Tiredness was probably a factor, his senses dulled, mind unable to cope with anything more than his own thoughts charging through his head. "No, but I can try."

He stood in the middle of what he assumed was a guest room, double bed in the centre, wooden wardrobe and matching beside cabinets the only other furniture. Pine, if he wasn't mistaken. Varnished a deep amber that bordered on orange. It looked cheap, considering the amount of money Cordelia had. He closed his eyes, clearing his mind of everything that filled it. The relief of that alone eased the ache in his shoulders, the tension squirting out of his muscles like toothpaste from a tube.

It came, a voice, whisper-soft and one he hadn't expected to hear.

"I'm outside."

"Shields?"

Langham spun around, eyebrows raised so high his eyes appeared lidless. "What the fuck?" he mouthed. "Jesus fucking Christ. This isn't something we need at the moment, a cop being killed. Riles all the other coppers. Damn man always did fuck things up."

"Shh! I don't want to lose him," Oliver said.

"Well! He winds me the hell up."

"He won't anymore, will he!"

"This is hard. Can't..."

"Hold on, Shields," Oliver said. "Relax. Concentrate only on speaking to me. Imagine you're just resting with your eyes closed, and speak, let the words come." Oliver's mind filled with questions, ones he didn't bloody need. He'd have to work hard to keep Shields with him if he wanted answers.

"Right. I'm sorry. For... I'm just sorry."

"Fuck being sorry. That crap doesn't matter anymore. Just tell me what you know."

"Cordelia, she isn't involved. Hasn't got a clue what's been going on. You hearing me okay? Is this working?"

"Yep. Go on."

"It's Robert, her new man. Passes him off as a chauffeur, not that I give a monkey's what he is. He's the one you want. The one who...who left me outside."

"What were you doing here?"

"I came to...to warn her. Went to see Mrs Roosay. She spoke to me through the letterbox. Told me the number plate of the car. I knew then...knew I should have said something about Cordelia owning Privo, that I didn't think she had it in her to be involved in something like this."

For Langham's benefit, Oliver repeated, "Mrs Rosé spoke to you through the letterbox?"

The detective blurted, "Oh, for fuck's sake!"

"Langham, testy as ever."

Oliver smiled. Then a thought struck him – hard. Ronan Dougherty had said one of the dead had lied to Oliver. Implied it had been Louise. Said the owner of Privo was the one they were after. Why had he lied? He asked Shields if he knew.

"Ronan knew about it from the start. Was friends with Robert."

"So why was Ronan killed?"

"He got greedy. Wanted more than a sixty-forty cut. He wanted the sixty. Said if he didn't get it he'd tell Cordelia the lot.

"Bastard lied to me. This just keeps getting worse!

Anything else we need to know?"

"*Glenn Close.*" Shields chuckled. "*She's planning on going to Mrs Roosay's later. Can't imagine the girl will harm the old woman, but you never know.*"

"Shit."

Oliver quickly relayed the news to Langham, who barked orders into his phone, "Send officers to ninety-seven Bridgewater Road pretty fucking quick if someone isn't there already, and make sure you keep the old woman safe and someone sticks around to get a hold of that girl, got it?"

"So why were you kil... Why are *you* outside?"

"*Robert. He told Cordelia he'd sort everything. Led me into the garden. She doesn't know I'm...like this. Thinks we were only talking. When she came in after you knocked on the door, she stood at the patio doors, staring out at us. Was holding something. Her diary, I think. I waved, let her know everything was fine. Didn't...*" A sob interrupted his speech. "*Didn't want her to know I had no control at all, that Robert had a gun on me. Pride... Always had a problem with it. Always did think I knew best. Shit. He waited until she'd gone before he pulled the trigger.*"

"We didn't hear a gunshot."

"*Silencer. Sounded like a damn puff of wind.*"

"Where is he now?"

"*I tried to follow, after...after... Saw him wade through the river. He had a car waiting, some guy in it I hadn't seen before. He told me when we were speaking... Said he kept the drug formula in his head, knew exactly how to get the strands made elsewhere if the shit hit the fan here. Fake passports, the lot. He'll be long gone. Private jet, so he said.*"

Oliver repeated the information so Langham could alert the airports, then asked Shields, "So what now? Do we have everyone except this Robert?"

"*Yes, him and the man who picked him up. The ones who made the drugs had no idea what they were doing. Thought it was just another part of their job.*"

"And the kids? Are there more than those we found in Reynolds' grandmother's basement?"

"No. Just them. From what I've gleaned from nosing about in this…state…you'll have Glenn soon. Unless she changes her mind about seeing Mrs Roosay."

"What about the eyes? The weird glowing eyes?"

"I was just going to get to that. Be careful. Robert isn't right."

"What do you mean?"

"I hate saying this to you, you know that? Even me being like… this…doesn't stop old habits dying hard. I'm a self-righteous bastard. Don't want you being right. Don't want you seeing me as anything like I am out there, but there's nothing I can do about that now. The state of me…"

"Forget all that. Just tell me what we need to know. No time for bullshit like that now."

A gusty sigh blew through Oliver's mind, making him think Shields had been sucked away, but his voice came loud and clear.

"Robert isn't human."

* * * *

"He's taking the piss, right?" Langham led the way outside, stride long and brisk. "Messing with us even now. How the *fuck* can someone not be human?"

"I don't know, all right? I'm just telling you what he said. He buggered off after he said that. He might not have meant it literally. We say shit like 'You're mental!' but it doesn't mean that person is mental. Know what I mean?"

"Yep, I do, but Shields should know better than saying shit like that then fucking off. I'm telling you, he's having a last little laugh on us. Bloody tosser."

In the garden, Oliver stood on a stretch of patio. Officers milled about, seemingly unsure as to what they were looking for.

"Body out here," Langham shouted. "Keep looking."

The policemen woke up, alert now they had something specific to search for. Oliver, although drained from his conversation with Shields, reached out to see if someone, anyone would give him any indication of where Shields' body was. Water, the image sharp and clear, filled his mind. He felt the rush of it over his skin, cold and startling, the weave of a fish as it flapped past.

"The river. Reckon he's in there," he said.

Langham sped off, his vigorous pace taking him to the end of the garden in seconds. Oliver ran after him, out of breath by the time he reached his side. They stared down an embankment at the river, a rushing, gambolling mass of frothy water, the current mean and unforgiving.

"Can't see a damn thing in this fading light," Langham complained. "And the spume isn't helping much either. Like a rowdy damn ocean down there. What's up with that?"

"No idea."

"Well, we need to check it out, whether we like it or not. Fuck's sake," he said as he navigated the slash of embankment. "Last thing I expected was going out to find Shields' sorry, tight arse."

"Hope that's figurative speech and not from intimate knowledge," Oliver said, following him down the hill.

"Damn right it is. I wouldn't fuck him if he was the last man on Earth." Langham laughed, reaching the bottom, pausing to catch his breath. "Shouldn't joke really. Officer killed in the line of duty and all that. Funny, but I'm relieved he wasn't involved. I'd begun to think he was."

Oliver stood beside him, lungs heavy from the chilly air. It was going to be a cold one tonight. "Me too. It pointed that way. And he was such an arsehole."

"Shouldn't speak ill of the dead." Langham walked towards the bank edge, moving his head left and right.

"Why not? I'm not going to say he was a good bloke just because he's dead. He wasn't. He was a wanker. Being dead doesn't change that."

"S'pose you're right. Shit."

"What?"

"There he is. I know I said you shouldn't speak ill, but..."

Langham laughed, bent over double, hands planted on his knees. It was the kind of laugh that bordered on hysteria.

"What's so funny? Where is he?" Oliver stared at the water, seeing nothing but rushing froth.

"There!" Langham pointed, wiping his wet cheeks.

Oliver gazed that way. Couldn't stop the smile that spread on his face, the chuckle that rumbled out of him. "Oh, fuck."

Shields' bare arse stuck out of the water, and nothing else.

"Seems this Robert has a sense of humour," Oliver said.

"Seems he does. Wouldn't have wanted to be him, though, pulling down those trousers."

"Me neither. Bit sick, don't you think?"

"A little, but hey, people do the strangest things." Langham used his phone, telling whoever was on the other line that they needed a team down here, forensics too. And how the fuck had the other officers missed a great big arse poking out of the river? He cut the call. "That body needs getting out of there fast. Photos taken. The way that river's going, it'll wash any evidence away."

"We don't even know Robert's surname," Oliver said.

"No, and that's something we need to find out." He called the station, using orders for some desk jockey to root out the information. He cut off the call. "Best part of my job, that."

"What is?" Oliver stared at Shields' arse. His vision blurred, mind weary of the constant battering it'd had all day, but not before he caught sight of something he'd rather not have.

"Having someone else do the dirty work."

"Seems like we've got enough dirty work of our own judging by that crack."

"Crack?"

"Shields' arse crack. He shit himself before he died."

"Aww, fuck. Why did you have to go and point that out? Christ. I feel sorry for him now."

Oliver sighed, and even though he hated to admit it, he

said, "Me too. Me fucking too."

* * * *

The call came in that one Robert Sanders and his companion, Peter Newbury, had been apprehended at the local airport. Robert had been a nightmare to contain, his strength that of ten men. It had taken several officers to apprehend him.

It wasn't a huge airfield, more a strip of land surrounded by grass and a pitiful excuse for a control tower, which lurched to one side as though the wind had pushed it a little too hard for a little too long. He'd been taken to the station, would be left in a cell over night until Langham could interview him in the morning. He didn't have time now — they were on their way to Mrs Rosé's, having received word that Glenn Close had been spotted at the park opposite the row of houses in her street. According to an officer hiding in Mrs Rosé's front garden, Glenn was flying high on a swing and had been for the past five minutes. And according to Sanders, Glenn hadn't returned to him after she'd killed her parents, as he'd instructed. She was surrounded on all sides, officers ready to catch her in case she bolted.

"Damn shame, that, when you think about it," Langham said.

Oliver nodded, staring out of the windshield at a now dark sky, thinking of Glenn. He saw her on a swing in his mind's eye, hair flying behind her as she surged forward, the length of it streaming over her face as she flew back. She was doing what she always should have, being a kid with no cares in the world except when her dinner was ready and whether she could have sweets afterwards. Except she hadn't ever had that kind of life, had she? Shitty parents had denied her the childhood she had deserved, the pair of fucking bastards.

Yeah, Oliver acknowledged that his anger towards Mr and Mrs Close was probably stronger because he'd had a strained and unhappy childhood himself, knew a little of what Glenn had gone through. Wished he'd been able to swing on the damn swings without constantly worrying he'd be called a weird little bastard or worse. And if he were honest, what they were about to walk into frightened him. He didn't want to see that kid taken away, treated like a criminal. He hoped the police who dealt with her were compassionate, understood why she'd acted as she had, that drugs had played a major part in what she had done. It was out of his hands, probably out of Langham's, too, but at least the detective could keep tabs on her, could let Oliver know how she fared after her fate had been decided.

What had happened to the other kids? They'd been taken to the hospital, he knew that, but when would they be reunited with their frantic parents? When all the tests on them had been exhausted? When it was deemed okay that they weren't a threat to society? He had no idea if any of them had killed. He hoped the only murderers were Alex Reynolds and Glenn. No other bodies had turned up, no new spirits had spoken to him, but that didn't mean jack shit.

Langham parked at the end of the street farthest from the park. They got out of the car, closing their doors quietly, and Langham locked them without using his electronic key fob, just the key. The *blip-blip-blip* of it would have been too loud in the quiet street, alerting Glenn that someone was about.

They didn't need her running. This needed to end. Now.

"How are you going to do this?" Oliver whispered, following Langham across the road to the side the park was on.

"I have no fucking clue. Instinct says just to go up to her, see what she does."

Oliver widened his eyes. "What? And risk her going for you?"

"She didn't go back to Robert Sanders, so my guess is the drugs will have worn off by now."

133

"But what if they haven't? What if she's still crazed?"

"I don't know, man. Maybe I'm not thinking straight. Maybe I should be armed. Who the fuck knows?"

"At least talk to her from the other side of the fence first."

An iron-railing fence skirted the park, enclosing it as a child's oasis, supposedly keeping them safe from weirdoes or them running out into the path of a car on Bridgewater Road. Fences didn't stop anyone if they had a mind to do something, and from what Glenn had done, she might have a mind, all right.

They came to a stop, level with that little girl coasting through the air. Two street lamps burned brightly, illuminating the apparatus. Illuminating her. She had a glazed look about her, stare glassy, just one kid going through the motions of making the swing move. No enjoyment, nothing.

"She's come down off the high," Langham said. "Reckon I'm safe to go in?"

Oliver shook his head. "I don't know, man. Is it wise?"

"I'll be all right, you know." Langham looked at him and smiled, but he appeared tense, like he was withholding something.

"What's going on?" Oliver asked, swallowing to wet his suddenly dry throat.

"The park's surrounded, right?"

"Right."

"With trained marksmen."

"*What?*"

"Sounds mad, doesn't it? Guns needed for a little kid. But there's no telling what state she's in, and kid or not, she's got to be taken into the city somehow. If she turns feral, well…"

Oliver held his hand up. Didn't want to hear anymore. "Right. But I'm coming with you."

"Not a good idea. You're not trained for this crap."

Oliver glanced at Glenn. She seemed to have no clue they were there.

Swing-swing-swinging.   Hair   whoosh-whoosh-whooshing.

"I still want to come."

"I could get in shit for letting you."

"Right."

"So I'll get in shit if I have to, so long as you get the fuck away if she flies off on one, you got that? I don't want you hurt."

Wrong place, wrong time. Again. Oliver wanted to bury his face in Langham's neck, kiss the stubble on his cheek, have it hurt his lips. "And when she's been taken to the hospital, we're out of here. Right? No way can they expect you to work more hours. Not after what we've been through since last night."

"Right. So let me get the kid, have her secured."

"Okay. Yeah, okay." Oliver nodded decisively. "But I'm still coming with you."

Langham sighed. "You infuriating little bitch."

"That's me. Deal with it."

Langham allowed a small smile then pushed open the metal gate. The hinges protested with a whine so harsh it hurt Oliver's ears. He cautiously trailed the detective, gaze fixed on Glenn, who still swung high. A slight movement from her head, and she began to slow, holding her legs out in front of her, stuck together, toes pointed in dirty white pumps, laces hanging.

They reminded Oliver of Louise's boots, what with the laces being undone, and he shuddered.

By the time they reached the swing, Glenn was still, feet on the ground, hands gripping the metal chains either side of her. Blood stained her — everywhere, everywhere — and he was surprised someone hadn't noticed that. Where the hell had she been since killing her parents? If someone *had* seen her, had they been stupid enough to think she was swathed in *paint?* Had they been so fixated on their own lives they hadn't seen that this kid needed help? He shook his head, uncaring that tears stung his eyes and that marksmen might see them fall. He felt for this child, deep inside him where he felt the most, in his heart, right down in the centre of it.

"Glenn?" Oliver said.

She turned her head slowly, eyes the colour of a boisterous, storm-laden sky. Grey and bleak. No spark. No joy. Shit, he wanted to gather her in his arms and squeeze some damn love into her, let her know someone cared. Her face, Christ, it was near black with dried blood, flecks of it flapping in the slight breeze, breaking free to jostle in the air, then disappearing into the surrounding darkness.

She stood, swivelled to face them.

Oliver did what came naturally and held out his arms.

And Glenn ran into them.

"Hold your fire!" Langham shouted.

Glenn clutched Oliver tightly about the back, the squall of her heart-wrenching sobs tearing a massive rip in his soul.

Chapter Fourteen

They were finally 'someplace', a nondescript building, one of those efforts that had sprouted up all over the country in recent years. The kind that stood on the outskirts of towns and cities, brazenly edged motorway petrol stations shouting 'Look at me!' with windows all the same little slits, facades boring to the eye, nothing remarkable here, folks. Where you paid thirty quid for the night, a clean bed, a small bathroom, a bit of breakfast, and that was that. No frills.

No frills suited Oliver down to the ground. He was fucking knackered, to put it mildly, and wanted nothing more than a shower, something to eat and to begin his long-awaited date with Langham. He kicked his shoes off, removed his socks, and oddly, as he stood in the centre of the room, feet naked, bed to his right, bathroom to his left, he felt awkward. Suddenly shy. Stupid. Out of his depth. For the past six months he'd coveted the detective, wished him in his arms, in his bed, in his arse, yet now it was about to happen, he was unexpectedly shunted into insecurity. And that bastard insecurity enclosed him, wrapping itself around him, inside him, every-damn-where until he struggled to breathe.

"You okay?" Langham asked, stripping off his clothes like he'd done it in front of Oliver a million times.

To be like that. To be so at ease with yourself...

"Uh, yeah. Bit nervous." His heart beat fast, pulse pounding in his ears, meshing with his heavy breaths.

"Of me?" Langham stopped undressing, stood there in his tight grey boxers, the bulge in his pants making Oliver more nervous than ever. "Fuck off!"

Oliver laughed a little, tension floating away only to return when Langham yanked down his boxers and kicked them away. That cock — *Jesus Christ!* — hard and long, jutted away from the detective's belly and bobbed. The size and weight of it held Oliver in awe, squished his stomach muscles tight and lengthened his own cock.

Langham was so out of Oliver's league.

"You like?" Langham asked, holding his hands out by his sides, palms up.

Did. He. Like?

"Fuck, yes!"

Oliver stared at the rest of him, unable to say anything more or make a move towards the man. A smattering of hairs coasted across Langham's chest, tapering down in a thicker band towards his navel. It expanded beneath, spreading across and down to the thick-as-fuck bunch at the top of his dick, darker and coarser than those everywhere else. Oliver wanted to kneel, to bury his nose in it and take in the scent of him. The thought of it hurt his dick as it expanded sharply, a huge strain of pulsing hardness pulling his skin taut.

Balls, heavy and large, hung between Langham's partially opened legs, ripe for sucking into Oliver's mouth, for his tongue to swirl all over them, making them wet. His own bollocks surged up, his arsehole puckering in tandem, and he clenched his hands into fists to stop himself rushing forward. He was conscious of his own smell, of the sweat that had dried, soaked and dried several times over in the past few hours. He didn't want Langham taking him like that, when he was dirty and carried the stench of death with him. His mouth felt like the bottom of a bird cage too, nasty, tacky spittle, tongue arid and thick. He didn't want to kiss him like that, touch him like that.

He shifted his gaze downward, to legs that had carried Langham from crime scene to crime scene, possibly going wobbly when he saw something horrendous, holding him more upright when he needed to be authoritative. The thigh muscles were pronounced, the shape of ancient, elongated spearheads, and Oliver itched to run his tongue up them, the hairs grating his chin.

Quickly, he looked higher, skating over that cock, one he'd swear had grown bigger, to shoulders that would mould perfectly beneath his palms. To a neck, tendons strained and corded, that he could run his tongue up and down, tasting Langham's day, where he'd been, what he'd done. His jaw, rigid, the stubble daring to be named a beard now, and a square-based chin he imagined brushing his bollocks as Langham licked his cock.

Oh, God, he needed that shower.

"You finished?" Langham asked, the teasing smirk on his lips spreading into a wider smile.

"Um, yep. I just… I should shower." Oliver lifted his arm, pointing towards the bathroom, and shuffled sideways, unable to take his gaze from Langham's face. "A bit hot. Dirty."

"I thought that was the whole idea. Getting hot and dirty."

How the hell did he stand there like that, at ease, so comfortable, when Oliver felt so damned exposed? And he wasn't even undressed! He may as well have been. Langham's gaze had stripped him naked, seen beneath his T-shirt, his jeans that could stand up by themselves if he took them off they were that rigid with dried sweat and the day's worth of dirt.

"It was. Is. I just…"

Oliver bolted, Langham's hearty laughter soaring after him, and slammed the bathroom door. He felt so bloody stupid, must have looked a right prick running in here like that. With his back pressed to the door, he fumbled to the side, intending to lock it so he could gather his wits. But Langham might take that as a rebuff if he tried to come in, and really, Oliver wanted the man to follow him. Yes, despite his belly doing somersaults and his knees going weak, he damn well wanted Langham to come in here and make everything all right.

Langham gave the impression he was experienced. In the office earlier, when he'd covered Oliver's hand with his, had spoken those words into his ear, he'd shown Oliver he was a man who knew what he was doing, knew what flirting was all about. How many men had he been with to get like that? Or was he just a natural seducer? Compared to him, Oliver was a novice, unversed, unsure, unworthy, so fucking *un* at everything except listening to the dead.

Useless prick, that's what you are. Can't even get this right.

A knock on the door startled him shitless, and he jumped, stifling a bark of surprise just in time. Last thing he needed was Langham knowing just how scared he was. How inexperienced. Oliver had been with men, of course he had, but they had been mere fumbles, testing the waters, hasty fucks at the end of drunken nights. No real relationships. No sex with anyone who actually knew what they were doing. That was frightening, knowing Langham knew all the right things to say, the right moves, the right everything. Would he be willing to teach? Be patient? To show Oliver the way?

"Can I come in, man?" Langham asked, voice muffled through the white-painted wooden door.

Could he?

"Uh, yeah. Hang on." Oliver sucked in a deep breath then moved away from the door. "Okay. It's okay." Was he reassuring himself there? Probably.

No probably about it, you fucking pansy. Grow some damn balls.

He busied himself switching on the shower, his back to the door as it opened. He set the temperature, fussing for far too long with the dial and holding his hand beneath the water. Langham was patient, Oliver would give him that. He saw him from the corner of his eye, filling that doorway like sardines in a tin, packed right up to the edges, no room for manoeuvre.

"You want out of this?" Langham asked, voice strong, as though he'd steeled himself for a negative answer.

"Fuck no!" Oliver blurted quickly, whipping his head around to face him. "It's just... Shit, we get along, right? I can fuck about with you, winding you up, piss-arsing about, and I'm comfortable with that, yeah? But in your office, in the car, when you get close..." He struggled to find the right words—words that wouldn't give Langham the wrong idea. He gave in and just said how he felt. "I'm shitting myself, all right?"

"Shitting yourself?"

"Yeah."

Steam started filling the small room, trying to push past the miniscule gaps around Langham. His cock was still hard, standing upright instead of outward now, those balls of his hanging lower than they had before.

"What about? Shitting yourself about what?"

Oliver's face heated, and it wasn't from the steam. He felt stupid again. "You. Us. This."

"So I make you shit yourself?" He cocked his head.

Didn't he realise that just him standing there like...*like that*...made Oliver nervous as hell?

"Yeah. Stupid, right?"

"No. No. I must give out the wrong impression. I don't mean to."

Oliver smiled, feeling ridiculous and timid, wishing he hadn't said anything at all and had just gone with it, pretending he knew what the fuck this experienced business was all about. But he couldn't. It would mean lying, and he didn't want that. Not with Langham. No, never that with him.

"It's me. Never been with anyone like you before," he said, face burning hotter at his outburst. He needed to control his mouth as well as his thoughts, he knew that. Offended the damn dead and now Langham from the look on his face. He rushed on. "It's just that...I wanted it all to be so right, for me to be with you and know what the hell I was doing. Properly. But I don't."

Langham lifted one arm, gripped the top of the door, the

action showcasing muscles that Oliver wanted to smooth his hands over. Why didn't he just step forward and do that? Why didn't he just do what his instincts were screaming and take that sexy-as-fuck man in his arms, press his mouth to his, his cock to his, and go with the damn flow?

"It *will* be right. You *will* know what you're doing. Just relax."

"But I won't. I'll fuck it up like everything else."

"Oh, come on now. No pity party here, man. This is me, remember? The guy you've spent six months working with. The guy you rip the piss out of on an almost daily basis. I never would have guessed from the way you act you'd feel like this. I thought... Shit, I thought you'd been around the block a few times, knew what you were doing. If I'd have known... Fuck, I'd never have come on to you in the office like that. I'm sorry, man."

"It's all right. Okay. I've just got to stop being such a prick. Grow up."

Langham looked at him, not with pity but with understanding. "You want to shower alone? Have a bit of space? And you don't have to do this when you get out, you know that, right?"

Oliver nodded, and Langham turned to leave.

"Stop," Oliver said. "Wait. I didn't mean... I didn't nod for you to go."

There, he'd said it. Had been assertive. If he put it off now, he didn't know if he'd ever have the courage to be in this position again. And if he let him go... What if he didn't come back?

Langham faced him again, stepping farther into the room. "You sure?"

"Yeah. I'm sure."

"You want me to join you or sit on the toilet and wait?"

"With the lid down, I hope."

Langham's laugh eased the tension inside Oliver. Just a bit.

"Damn right with the lid down. I might give the

impression I'm open to anything, but even I don't crap in front of a lover. At least not on the first date, anyway." He winked, grinned hard and wide. "Want some help getting undressed?"

Oliver took in a deep breath then released it through pursed lips. He nodded and closed his eyes, skin prickling as he waited for the first shift of clothing. Almost without sound, Langham came closer, the heat of his breath caressing Oliver's face. A shiver streaked wickedly down his spine, and he convulsed from the strength of it.

"I'm not that bad, am I?" Langham teased, gently easing Oliver's T-shirt up his chest.

"No. It's not that, it was—"

"Shh. I'm messing."

"Oh."

Oliver lifted his arms to allow Langham to finish removing the shirt. Steam encompassed him, cloying and hot, and he wondered if he'd set the temperature too high. Wondered if Langham liked it cool or boiling. Whether he would step into the shower with him and explore his body like he wanted him to. Wanted yet didn't. It was all so exciting, so terrifying, he didn't know what the hell he wanted.

"If you just calm down," Langham said, unbuttoning Oliver's jeans, "you'll find this a lot more pleasurable. Pretend you're dreaming, if you like. You do dream about me, right?"

Even though Oliver had his eyes closed, he knew damn well Langham was smiling. That tone of voice, the one he used every day when they fucked about, rang out as clear as the peal of Sunday church bells.

"Yeah, you got me," he managed, swallowing hard.

"Ah, good. Can't have you not dreaming. Not wanting."

Oliver's stomach flipped, his cock springing free of his boxers as his man drew them and his jeans down his legs. Something brushed his cock—Langham's hair? Was he kneeling? Down *there?*—and it swelled harder, the swiftness of it filling almost painful.

"You smell good," Langham said.

Oliver swallowed again, stepping out of his clothes as they reached his ankles, careful not to make a dick of himself by slipping on the condensation-covered floor. He didn't have the courage to open his eyes, not yet, so kept them closed and waited for what Langham would do next.

Nothing touched him, and he stood there all alone, naked, bared for Langham to drink in. If he was touched, at least he'd know where Langham was. But if he opened his eyes, what if he caught an expression of disgust on his face? What if Langham didn't like what he saw?

"Fuck, you're *nicely* turned out," Langham said, the appreciation in his tone something even Oliver couldn't brush off.

Relief swept through him, and he dared to crack open his eyes a touch. Through the grey steam, he saw Langham standing close, eyeing him up and down, hot-as-fuck grin pulling one corner of his mouth up. He wanted to laugh, too damn pleased the detective looked at him that way. *Him,* Oliver, Mr Inadequate in the Bedroom.

"Fucking gorgeous," Langham breathed. "And all mine."

Now *that* sent a surge of heated lust straight to Oliver's groin. He grinned, feeling so much better now, but not quite at the point of comfortable ease he wanted to be.

"You want some help in there?" Langham jerked his head towards the shower cubicle. "I give a mean wash."

Oliver nodded, stepping into the shower, conscious that his arse was on show and hoping it didn't have any blemishes. What the fuck was up with him, thinking like a girl? He ought to pack it in and just enjoy himself. Still, the thought persisted, nagging at him, laughing at him.

"Nice arse. *Very* nice arse."

Oliver's stomach rolled yet again. If he wasn't careful he'd throw up bile. This was too much — too exciting and too damn everything. He just needed to calm down like Langham had said. He moved over, hoping the bigger man would fit inside with him. He did — a snug fit, but that was okay, he could deal with that now. Langham wasn't touching him, but he was close enough to if he moved forward an inch. His body would press against Oliver's. His cock would too.

Lord, that cock touching his, touching any bloody part of him might make Oliver shoot his load too soon. He tilted his head back and closed his eyes, letting the water cascade over his face and seep into his mouth. He'd wanted to brush his teeth, to make the fuzz of the day go away, but warm water would have to do. Better than nothing.

The cold shock of shower gel on hot hands against his skin had his head snapping forward. He stared down at Langham's fingers, unable to meet his gaze. He needed a minute to adjust, to accept what Langham was doing. Those broad hands, they glided over his skin, white bubbles seeping between Langham's fingers, oozing down to coat his wrists. His touch, so soft yet firm, sent Oliver's pulse racing. The lump on his head from the car accident ached a little, as did his finger, but he pushed the discomfort aside. His heart *hurt*, damn it, beating too fast like that, throbbing inside a too-tight chest. His ribs seemed to squeeze his lungs, pushing out the air they contained and refusing to allow any more in. Oliver gasped, jump-starting his lungs to work again, and they inflated, the rush of air making him dizzy.

"You feel good," Langham said, moving his hands slowly, giving Oliver time to adjust to being touched this way.

A fluffy ribbon of soap slunk down Oliver's belly, seeping into his pubic hair, a featherlight swarm on the base of his cock. He wondered if Langham could touch him like that, with those hands as big as shovels, his strength held at bay. As though the detective had read his mind, he slid one hand downward and lightly grasped Oliver's dick. Oliver gasped, the curl of fingers around him sensuous and right, something he'd never thought he'd feel. Hell, dreams, they were one thing, but reality was another. How had he struck so lucky? How was it he was staring down at that hand, his dick, the man he'd dreamt about in the shower with him?

It was happening, wasn't it, this wish of his? For real?

"All right?" Langham asked.

Finally, *finally* Oliver found the courage to look up. He nodded, hands useless by his sides, itching to curve his fingers around Langham's length. Could he do that? Really? Now?

Before he could stop himself, he lifted one hand, gaze fixed on Langham's face. The detective, he bared his essence, those eyes of his inviting Oliver in, through the windows and into his soul. Something happened then, a subtle shift of emotion that hummed between them, and as Oliver drew his hand up, snaked it between them and held that wide, hefty cock, he knew he was safe.

He'd found home.

Chapter Fifteen

Fresh from the shower, the heat of the pattering water and Langham's touch still zinging over his skin, Oliver left the bathroom. Langham had left before him, going into the bedroom, giving Oliver a glimpse of his arse for the first time. He hadn't dared look whilst they'd been in the shower, or as Langham had stepped out, their soft encounter under the stream still making him reel. He'd needed a few seconds to compose himself, pinch his arm to make himself accept this was real. Oh, the way he'd been touched was real all right, he knew that, but the experience was so *sur*real he had trouble processing it.

In the bathroom doorway, he looked across the bedroom at Langham, who was at the open, head-height window, body shielded from any prying eyes. Oliver was glad — he didn't want anyone else looking at his man, seeing him like that. Like Langham had said — '*And all mine.*'

That arse, he appraised it now, taking in the swell of each cheek, the deep cleft between them, all shadows and mystery inside. What would it feel like to part them, to peek in there at the pucker he'd long wanted to pierce, the heated sheath tight and relentless around him? Langham struck him as a man who liked to be inside another — would he want to take turns? There was so much he didn't know about him, so much yet to learn. Okay, he had a good handle on his personality, his sharp wit, the fact that he cared a lot about his job and doing it right. But what of personal things? Yeah, Langham liked pizza with too many onions for Oliver's tastes, and cheese toasties with barely enough cheese to make it worthwhile, but those kinds of things weren't what he wanted to know.

Was he a morning person or a night owl? Was he happiest spending his free time reading, watching TV, or did he have some wild and whacky things he did, like extreme sports? How could Oliver work with him and not know anything like that?

He wanted to find out. Know every bloody thing about him.

"I know you're watching," Langham said.

"How?"

"I can see your reflection in the glass. See the way it slants because it's open? Been watching you too. You've got yourself one damn fine body there."

For fuck's *sake!* Did that man know *all* the right things to say? Oliver's ego boosted, fear and worry scuttling off to the far recesses of his mind, and his muscles relaxed—muscles he hadn't even been aware were scrunched tight.

"Got a fine damn body yourself," he said, inordinately happy the words didn't falter, didn't sound stupid, make him *feel* stupid. They fitted somehow, in this time, this room, with Langham facing away from him like that. Maybe that was Oliver's problem. Being close, naked, the detective scrutinising him with that raking gaze of his... Maybe Oliver just needed Langham unable to see him for now. Well, Langham could see him in the window, but that was all right. It wasn't so blatant, his image wasn't so real.

Oliver walked up behind Langham, shitting bricks yet at the same time drowning in courage. That wasn't right—to feel two opposing emotions like that wasn't possible. Yet it was, because he felt them right now, warring with one another, courage urging him to take matters into his own hands and see where it took them, the shit bricks, those stinking, hateful bricks jeering that he didn't have the bollocks to see this through.

I do. I fucking well do.

He reached Langham, faltered for a moment, hands partially lifted, held in place mid-air by a bluff attack of

148

indecision. He lowered them and stared at Langham's back, eyed the spritz of freckles, so light they were hardly there, then let his gaze rise, settling on the nape of his neck. An upside down question mark of hair rested in the centre, so damp the base of the curve was bloated with shower water. It fled its anchor, dropped onto his skin and zigzagged down his back, losing its bulbous size the farther it travelled until it was nothing.

That wet strip. Oliver wanted to lick it.

"Do whatever it is you're thinking of doing," Langham said, startling Oliver from his perusal. "Just do it. I don't bite."

Oliver would have usually retorted 'Much!' but this time he didn't. If he spoke it would break the spell, one he'd cast while standing there, soaking up the sight of this man, something he couldn't imagine tiring of. So he leant forward and licked that wet line from the bottom of Langham's back to the curl of hair it had dripped from. He drew away an inch, breaths fanning back at him after hitting the nape of Langham's neck, and waited for more instincts to come, to tell him what to do. Or for Langham to make a move, a noise, anything that indicated Oliver had done the right thing.

Nothing came, and he panicked for a moment, wanting to run back into the bathroom and hide there until morning. But his cock ached, he needed release, and if he legged it he might never get another chance like this again.

"If you're still unsure," Langham said, "we can leave it for another time. No rush. I'm not going anywhere. Plenty of time."

If Oliver looked at the window, he'd see Langham looking back at him, he was sure, so he closed his eyes and lifted his hands again, hoping they would land where he wanted them to and he wasn't left looking like a complete dickhead, blindly waving his arms about. Relieved when his palms touched Langham's waist, Oliver slid his hands across, over that stomach he'd admired earlier, feeling out the rippled abdomen, the way each muscle was a tight square. Higher still, he ran his fingers through the coarse hair on the detective's chest, thrilled by the tickle on his skin. Daring, he rested his cheek against Langham's smooth shoulder blade and opened his eyes to stare at the wall, seeing nothing but feeling everything. Emotions, they were a strange bunch, careening through him, bringing on nausea, exhilaration and a whole heap of other things that, combined, made him lightheaded and slightly shaky.

Scooting his body closer, he found the courage to press himself to Langham, his cock settling in the shadowy arse cleft like it was made to do so. The contact nearly had him crying out, and he bit his lip to stop any stupid noises leaving him without permission. How long had he wanted this? Too bloody long, and now it was here, he couldn't quite believe it.

Langham's hands covered his, and Oliver jolted from the unexpected touch. With his man guiding him, Oliver sucked in the feel of hairy skin, the bump of a nipple as one hand coasted over it. And he was directed down, back across the muscle squares and lower, until wiry pubic hair grazed the sides of his hands.

"Touch me," Langham said, "right…there."

Oliver's hand met Langham's cock. His own dick stiffened, nestling farther inside the cleft as though getting comfortable. Oliver squeezed his eyes tighter, held his free hand against a hip bone he could imagine licking one day, the skin salty.

"Hold it," Langham said.

Oliver obeyed, curling his fingers around the hot shaft with more than a little anxiety streaming through him. His heart pattered, *whumping* with accelerated speed. He swallowed to combat his nerves, then grew brazen enough to grip harder. It throbbed in his hand, the vein beating in time with his heart, and he thought of how it would smell, fresh from the shower, his nose buried in the hairs surrounding it.

Langham took his hand away, left Oliver to it, hanging both arms by his sides. Given the green light to explore, Oliver slid his lightly clenched fist up Langham's dick, taking the foreskin with it. He eased it back down, pulling as far as he could before repeating the upward motion. Again and again. Again and again.

Langham gasped, a small moan following.

Oliver reached down with his other hand to try to cup the man's balls. His fingertips met their fuzz-covered softness, but his arm wasn't long enough to do what he wanted. Langham was as broad as Oliver was slight. Instead, he gave Langham's cock a soft double grip, moving his hands up and down slowly so he could learn the shape of him, how his cock responded. Expanding in his hands, Langham's length felt sexy as fuck, and Oliver pressed himself even closer until his chest touched Langham's back, breaths growing heavy, fractured.

"It looks hot, what you're doing," Langham said.

Oliver opened his eyes and, before he could talk himself out of it, lifted his face to peer around Langham's arm. In the window reflection, he saw his hands moving slowly up and down, the head of Langham's cock fat and wide, peeking out each time he drew down. He salivated, longing to flick the end with his tongue, take that cock into his mouth and suck long and slow. Taste pre-cum and keep sucking until the real prize gushed out.

"Feels good, but…" Langham eased Oliver's hands away and turned to face him, drawing him close so their dicks squashed together. He ran his hands up and down Oliver's biceps and looked down into his eyes. "It's time to move over to the bed."

Oliver's stomach contracted, and he averted his gaze, Langham's eyes too penetrating for him to look at much longer. They seemed to know him already, dip right inside his mind, and he wondered if Langham had studied him over the past few months more than Oliver had thought. Belly in tighter knots, he stepped back as Langham pushed him using his body, until the backs of Oliver's knees met with the edge of the mattress. Oliver folded. Letting himself fall down, back to the bed, his calves dangling over the edge, he wiggled his toes in the carpet pile. Langham stared down at him, eyes full of want, and clutched the cock Oliver had so recently fondled.

"Doesn't feel the same," Langham said, sliding his hand up and down. "Just doesn't feel the same." He let go then climbed on the bed, the mattress dipping. He straddled Oliver on hands and knees, face now level with his. "I want you. Want all of you on me, in me, over me. Reckon you can handle that?"

Oliver nodded, his chest feeling hollow except for a heart that thrummed loud and hard. His body had gone suddenly numb, heavy, as though the adrenaline and excitement speeding through him had prevented all movement. He went to lift one hand, his arm leaden and stiff, then let it fall back to the bed.

"I… Fuck, I'm…"

"I'll take over. Just stay there. You're too tired for much." Langham took a moment to rake his gaze over Oliver, from his face down to his cock and back again. "Damn fine. *Damn* fine."

He lowered his head, giving Oliver a searing kiss, tongue probing, hot and wet and fucking divine. Oliver responded, managing to lift the arm that had refused to budge before, curving his hand around Langham's neck and holding him close. Shit, his cock *ached*, and he lifted his hips, wanting more of Langham's touch. Langham lay over him, deepening their kiss while rubbing his cock against Oliver's. The soft abrasion sent shocks of pleasure from Oliver's tightening balls right to the tip of his dick, and he felt pre-cum pool then drizzle. It wouldn't be long before he exploded, a mass of burning, sticky cum. Langham pressed his abdomen down, grinding hard into him, shifting his hips quickly as he kissed harder, faster.

The telltale bunching of Oliver's balls told him he'd

reached the point of no return, and he cursed his inability to wait longer. That he was finally here, in bed with Langham, kissing him, having him over him, their cocks together, was too much. He raised his other arm, grasping at Langham's neck as though he needed him to survive, and raised his head as much as he could, wanting the detective to know that he poured everything he had into that kiss. Love, respect...more, he wanted more of this, of everything. Langham worked faster, the friction from their cocks bringing on a burning sensation that streaked around Oliver's glans. With Langham's downward pull, Oliver's foreskin went with it, stretched tauter than any time he'd touched himself, and the slight pain of it was something else.

He whimpered into Langham's mouth, gripped his neck tighter, and his groin jerked as he pushed up to get more of that feeling, more of the burn. Dick throbbing, growing in length and width, Oliver couldn't hold back any longer. A surge of cum travelled up his cock, bursting out of him, cock hole stretching with the force. He wrenched his mouth away, turning to the side and crying out, his voice hoarse and broken. Langham fucked on with frantic, jerky thrusts, and lowered his head to Oliver's neck. He kissed and suckled, licked and nibbled. Another shot exploded, hot cum making Langham's dick glide, the sensations different from the dryness. More erotic. More...just more.

Oliver dug his fingertips into Langham's shoulders, bracing himself for a third expulsion that currently zipped up his cock. "Fuck! God. Oh, ah, fuck!"

It came, sending his body into convulsions, and Langham slid one hand beneath Oliver to hold him steady.

"Fuck, I'm coming...coming too...ah, fuck!"

Langham's cum joined Oliver's, hot as hell and lots of it. His groin spasmed, and he pulled Oliver closer so he could grind his cock harder. He jolted, jerked, looking down at where their bodies joined.

"Look at that," he gasped out. "Right...now. Would

you...fucking...look...at *that*."

Oliver looked down, saw how their dicks slipped and slid, his still hard, Langham's even harder, and shit, it was hot to see. Sticky cum, creamy, sticky cum, coated the pair of them, their cock heads, Langham's lilac, Oliver's red, butting one another. If he never saw another thing again, he'd take that sight with him as the last thing he'd seen — gladly.

Breaths coming too fast for him to manage, Oliver took in a deep lungful of air to try to sort himself out. Langham's breathing rasped as he slowed, still staring between them as though he couldn't stand to tear his gaze away. Sweat dripped down his temple, and Oliver reached up to wipe it away.

"Fucking hot," Langham said. "Cocks. Ours. So fucking *nice*, man."

"I'm sorry," Oliver blurted.

"For what?" Langham snapped his gaze up and looked at Oliver. "What the fuck for?"

"For being too quick. You know —"

"Man!" He shook his head, smile wide. "I mean this in the best possible way, but shut the fuck up, all right? It was perfect. Fast and wild. Perfect."

"Oh, I —"

"No, don't want to hear it. There'll be other times. This time was just right." He dipped his head, kissed Oliver softly, then drew back. "Like that. Fucking perfect."

Oliver smiled, conscious of the mess between them, the edges drying quickly making his skin itch. But he didn't want to push Langham away, have space between them. Langham took the matter into his own hands, though, crawling backwards off the bed and taking Oliver with him, leading him into the bathroom. He switched the shower on, stepping inside the stall before it had the chance to heat up, tugging Oliver to join him.

The cool water was a blessing on Oliver's overheated skin, and he closed his eyes for a moment, willing his heart to resume its usual pace. He felt like he'd run a mile, sweat popping out of his pores, the water thankfully sluicing it away. Chest tight, he opened his eyes again.

Langham stared at him, crooked smile lifted at one corner. "Okay?"

"More than."

Once again Langham washed him, took his time over it too, hands skating everywhere, exploring. A wider smile transformed his face when he scooped Oliver's balls in his hand, the shower gel frothing to obscure any view of bollocks on palm. Langham looked good wet, with droplets of water on his shoulders like that, the hairs on his chest flattened into dead-straight lines. He continued fondling, sliding his finger along the ridge between Oliver's sac and arsehole then back again. Holding his breath as he found his puckered hole and lingered, Oliver willed the man to breach the barrier. He did, popping his fingertip inside. Oliver widened his legs, a blatant invitation, and studied the top of Langham's head as he watched himself pushing his finger deeper. The bubbles from the soap stung.

"You like that?" the detective asked, looking at Oliver while easing in some more.

Oliver nodded.

"You like...that?" he said, pushing down on Oliver's prostate and circling over it.

Oliver gasped, nodded again and flashed one hand out to brace himself on the tiled wall. His cock twitched, the stirrings of new hardness beginning, and as Langham returned his gaze to what he was doing, Oliver rested a hand on the man's head and closed his fingers into a fist. Langham's hair was all kinds of bloody wonderful in his hand, and knowing he pulled it, had it straining at the roots, made his dick spring up again pretty damn quick.

"Yeah, I see you like that."

Langham kneeled, sucking Oliver's cock into his mouth so fast he barely had time to process it. The head hit the back of Langham's throat, teeth lightly scraping down the length, and it was all Oliver could do to keep himself from shouting out. This man was experienced, no doubt about it, knew exactly how much pressure to apply when sucking, exactly how hard to push inside his arsehole. The circular movements back there grew faster, then Langham changed tack, pushing his finger in and out, slipping another finger in beside it and scissoring to aid expansion. Oliver couldn't spread his legs wide enough, quickly enough, and the constant sucking on his cock would tip him over the edge if he didn't watch it.

Drawing up, Langham let Oliver's cock pop from his mouth and stood, finger still pumping his arse. "You want to turn around? So I can *really* see what I'm doing?" He eased his finger out, helping Oliver to face the back wall. "Put your hands up on the tile, lean into them."

He did, jutting his arse out and widening his legs so the sides of his knees touched the glass on one side and the tiled wall on the other. He wanted Langham in him so much he could taste it.

"We're clean, yeah?" Langham said.

More of a statement than a question, and it had Oliver's mind twirling in all directions. He was asking permission to fuck…properly. Oliver nodded, knowing the cop wouldn't be dirty in his line of work, and Oliver certainly hadn't done anything that was cause for worry.

"Good. Good."

Langham inserted his fingers again, three this time if the thickness was anything to go by, and Oliver gritted his teeth through the stretch. Fuck, it burned, but fuck, it felt good. Then, without warning, those fingers pulled out and the tip of Langham's fat cock nudged at his arsehole. He pushed in so slowly, yet it still made Oliver's rim throb and ache. He hadn't been fucked there in a long time—too long to admit—and although it wasn't as painful as the first time, it hurt well enough. He ground his teeth again, couldn't help but release a throttled moan.

"You—ah, Jesus that feels good—you okay?" Langham

asked.

"Yeah. Just do it. Please, just...ah, that's good. Yeah, like that. Push inside like that."

Langham eased in with a little more force, filling Oliver to the hilt. Oliver's arms gave out, and he found himself pressed against the tiles, cheek squashed, feet sliding as he scrunched his toes to gain purchase on the bobbled bottom of the tray. Langham's body covered him, and he slid his hand around to grip Oliver's cock, jerking it in time with his own as he upped his speed.

"This is how it is," the detective said, panting. "This is how...the fuck...it is." He groaned, shoving into Oliver faster, harder, tightening his fist and pumping on Oliver's cock. "Right here, like...this. You and me. No one—ah, ah, fuck!—else. Just us, yeah?"

"Yes!" Oliver shouted, loving the hot burn of his cock being roughly handled so soon after his last ejaculation, loving the wretched burn in his arse even more.

"My cock...up your...arse. Me...fucking you. Only—ah-ah-ah—me. You...got...that?"

"Yes, yes!" Oliver stuck his backside out again, pushing into Langham.

"You make me so fucking horny. So...fucking...ready for you. Wanted you for ages, like this, my...cock"—he groaned loudly and worked faster—"inside you, and you"—he slammed in and out with more vigour—"taking every...fucking...bit of me. You should see what this looks like. Yeah, me sliding in and...out. Your tasty little arse, greedy, sucking me in." He panted again, short outbursts of air. "Come for me, Oliver."

Oliver's cock throbbed—he was going to come again, no order needed.

"Yeah, you know it," Langham said. "We're going to... come so damn...hard. You and me. Together. Yeah, fucking yeah. We've got this thing. We've— I'm going to... Hell yeah, I'm going to come."

Langham's words, the way he'd said them, sent Oliver's

mind spinning. He couldn't take it all in, this new eroticism, this way Langham had of pressing all the right buttons and making him want to come yet again. He came with a croaky shout, the repetition of, "Yes, yes, yes!" mingling with Langham's stuttered groans.

"That's right," Langham said. "We've got it. Fuck! Let's fuck it out of us."

Jesus Christ…

Cum hurtled out of Oliver, fast and without the usual spurts, one long stream of ropey cream that smacked onto the tile and didn't seem to want to stop. He yelled, words he didn't understand or hear properly, not even sure whether they came from him or Langham. He closed his eyes, neck tendons straining, legs threatening to give way as wet heat filled his arse and Langham shouted through his orgasm.

When his ejaculation receded, Oliver slapped his hand over Langham's, taking it away from his overused cock. Out of breath, he savoured the slowing of Langham's movement in his arse, his rim stinging from the stretch and the bite of cum. Langham stopped, pulling Oliver away from the wall and, remaining inside him, crossed his arms over Oliver's chest and belly.

He murmured, "Like I said, Oliver. This is it. You and me. We've *got* this thing."

Chapter Sixteen

Oliver roused but kept his eyes closed, hoping to drop back to sleep. His pillow crackled, and he frowned. It didn't usually crackle. Wasn't filled with down like this one. His was a foam affair that moulded to the shape of his head. Where was he?

He snapped his eyes open, and all the memories came flooding back. He was 'someplace', with Langham sprawled beside him, inches of space separating their bodies because, Oliver guessed, they were so used to sleeping alone. He turned on his side and studied the detective, the flickering light from the TV illuminating a body Oliver still couldn't believe he'd touched.

Oliver liked the possessiveness, the feeling of being owned, of someone wanting to care for him the way Langham did. Monogamous, just them, no one else involved. It was different, something he hadn't done before, and the thought of a proper relationship had him grinning in the semi-darkness, wanting to laugh so hard until his belly muscles hurt.

Could he do that? Did he have what it took to make a relationship work? He was dedicated enough, and he cared for Langham in a way he hadn't cared for anyone else, but what if they didn't get along as a couple? What if being together as well as working with one another put a fuck-off spanner in the works?

A sudden, perceptible shift in his mood — the swift removal of happiness replaced by unease — had him bolting upright. His chest tightened, and he found it difficult to pull in a decent breath. He cocked his head, thinking, hoping the action would help him realise what was wrong. Something was, and he was sure it didn't have anything to do with what he'd just been thinking. It went deeper than that. With only the faint hum of God knew what out in the corridor and Langham's steady breathing, he couldn't fathom what the fuck was up. Was someone lurking outside their room? Who the hell knew they were here anyway?

A wave of cold swept over him, and he settled back on the bed, drawing the quilt up to his chin. His teeth chattered, the air turning cold, and a nasty pinch in the pit of his stomach was all the proof he needed that it wasn't someone or something in *this* life giving him the jitters.

"Who are you?" he whispered, the thought entering his mind that one of those God-awful demons had picked tonight to make a visit. He'd hated it the last time he'd seen one—it had freaked him out for days afterwards, ruining any chance he'd had of a decent night's sleep for well over a week. "What do you want?"

"I heard you're the one who can help me. You know, because I'm dead."

The voice wasn't faint or reedy, full of fear or puzzlement that the spirit had found themselves dead. No, this one was full of bravado, confidence, and had possibly belonged to a male arsehole in life.

"Yeah, I was an arsehole. Still am."

Oliver didn't feel badly that he hadn't shielded his thoughts this time. It seemed to him the man would prefer honesty.

"Yep. So here's some honesty from me. Nice to finally meet you properly, Oliver."

"Who are you?" he said again, louder but not loud enough to wake Langham.

"Mr Weird Eyes."

Alex bloody Reynolds.

He laughed—shards of glass splintering, then sandpaper on roughly hewn wood—the sound grating right on Oliver's nerves.

"Shut the fuck up," he snapped. "What do you want with me?"

"Nothing."

"Nothing? So fuck off then!" Oliver glanced over at Langham to make sure he still slept.

"Aww, that's no way to talk to someone who's just reaching out, wanting contact with someone he kinda knew in life. It's boring here, wherever the fuck I am. Dark place, trees every-damn-where. And the stink! It's like rotting veg."

"Jesus. I know where you are."

It was the same place as the other one, the demon who had visited him before, playing around with Oliver just because he could, just because the thin veil between worlds had allowed him through.

"You do? Well, aren't you going to tell me then?"

"It's a bad place, Alex. You're going to wish you weren't there." He paused, then a thought struck him. "Hang on, how the fuck did you *get* there?"

"Think I was going to spend the rest of my life in prison? Fuck, no. Coward's way out for me, man. I don't want no dirty faggot fucking me up the arse in the shower."

Oliver went cold. Had Alex been here when... No, Oliver would have felt him. Sensed it. "Shut the hell up. Just shut the hell up."

"Yeah, Shields said you were testy."

Shields had said that? In front of Alex? Jesus, the man had been such a bloody arsehole.

"Whatever, Alex. Look, tell me what you want. If you're only here to fuck me about, well, don't."

"Fine. See ya."

"Wait!" Oliver spoke louder than he'd intended, and whipped his head to the side to glance at Langham.

He slept on.

"What?"

"Your eyes. The kids' eyes. Contacts or real?"

"What, these eyes?"

A shadowy form manifested at the bottom of the bed,

hulking, menacing, the body shape that of a much bigger man than Alex had been. The glowing eyes appeared, wide and large, pupil-slits as long as a woman's fake fingernail, the irises the size of a two-pence piece. Oliver cried out, slapping one hand over his mouth. His legs went to jelly even though he was sitting, and his body felt like it had drained of everything solid, filling with a syrupy mass that pushed against his skin, wanting out.

"Oh, Jesus… No, not one of you again."

"Yeah, one of those, that's me. A devil in life, devil in death. I know exactly where I am. I was just messing with ya."

"Fuck off," Oliver said, trying to remember what he had to do to get rid of demons. He'd visited a channeller before, a woman who'd taught him how to only let the good ones in. After each time he'd spoken to the dead he was supposed to close himself off, imagine a cocoon covered him, no gaps, no way through the skin, keeping himself safe until the next time a spirit came knocking at his door. He was the one who was supposed to be in control, not them, and lately he'd forgotten the lesson, forgotten the ritual. How long had he left himself open like that? Months, probably.

Shit.

He imagined the cocoon growing from his feet to the top of his head, and chanted that the demon had to leave, wasn't welcome here. He wanted to close his eyes but didn't dare to in case Alex came closer. Touched him. Did something to him.

"There's one more out there. Just thought you should know. One more like me, getting ready to kill right…this…minute."

The shadow faded, the eyes dimming seconds later, and just as the cocoon reached the top of his head, before it had a chance to close and keep him secure, another spirit barged in.

"Wait! Let me speak! Don't go! Don't make me struggle to get you to hear me!"

Oliver abandoned the channelling, looking all around to make sure Alex had really gone. The unease he'd felt prior to the bastard coming had disappeared, but another chilling feeling had taken its place, white-hot in its intensity and not a pleasant sensation. Fingers of fear crept up his spine, and a strange, almost out-of-body-experience occurred. He wasn't 'someplace' anymore, but hovered above a bedroom, a double divan below with a woman on it, hacked to pieces, fresh blood still dripping from a corner of the bed sheet that hung over the side.

"You see me? You see me there?"

Oliver nodded.

"He's only just gone. You can catch him. I followed him. He's under the bypass, the one off Chaucer Street. He's… He's got… Oh, God, he's licking my blood off his hands."

"Where do you live? Where am I? Your flat?"

"Twenty-seven Portman Street. Bungalow with a green door."

"Your name?" Oliver couldn't look at her anymore, the blonde hair streaked red, the torso, arms and legs God knew where. Stomach gaping open, innards splayed across the bed like a bad impression of modern art.

"Sasha Morrison. He took parts of me. Has them with him. In a…black…refuse bag."

Oliver felt her pain, that her life had been cruelly ended, reduced to her being placed in bags designed to hold rubbish. "Why you? Do you know?"

"I'm the last one to know where the main man is. Who he is."

"The main man? There's another?"

"Yes. The two caught at the airport, they were just lackeys, men who acted like they'd masterminded the whole thing. They worked for someone else."

"Who?"

"Gideon Davis."

"Where is he?"

"Spain."

"Oh, Jesus. He runs the operation from there?"

"Yes. I… I need to go. I'm getting colder. It's…things are fading… W—"

Oliver went to call out, to ask her to hold on for a few

more seconds, but he was hauled from Sasha's flat and back onto the bed with Langham. As though he'd been thrown there, he bounced on his back, the mattress jostling beneath him. An arm clamped over his stomach, and he lashed out, freaked to fuck that Alex had been waiting for his return, a chance to get hold of him and do some serious harm. Oliver thrashed his arms and legs, a constant stream of "No, no, no!" leaving his mouth.

The arm pinned him down, then, "Hey, hey! Shh! It's me. You're just having a bad dream. Wake up!"

Langham's soothing voice calmed Oliver, and he let his body slump, curling towards the detective and burrowing into his embrace. Those strong arms took every bad thing away for a moment, leaving Oliver safe and protected, but then Alex and Sasha slammed into his mind again, and he drew back to look into eyes that held serious concern.

"What is it?" Langham asked.

Oliver babbled, spewing the last few minutes of events out into the air. Langham rubbed his back through the telling, no laughter or disbelief when Oliver said Alex had appeared as a demon. He hadn't expected that demon at all, not when he'd scoffed at the idea of glowing eyes and devils before.

"I swear to God, he was here. Right there at the end of the fucking bed. I'm not pissing about," Oliver said, easing back to sit up and fist his eyes. "Right fucking there." He pointed, mentally drawing the cocoon around him in case some other bastard devil had a mind to slip in without permission. "Those eyes. And the way he was. I can't believe he bloody killed himself."

"A lot of them do." Langham sat up beside him and continued rubbing circles at the bottom of Oliver's back. "They can't handle prison, yet they can handle killing people."

"It doesn't make sense. If you've got the guts to kill, why would prison freak you out?"

"Because they can't kill anymore. For most of them, killing

is in their blood."

"But Alex was made to kill. The drugs."

"I reckon, with him, he'd have killed eventually anyway. Wasn't your average human, was he?"

"No." Oliver sighed. "You going to call Sasha's death in?"

Langham nodded, then got off the bed and grabbed his phone. He dialled, speaking quickly, his words tripping over one another as he gave the location of the man who had killed Sasha and where they could find her body. He ended the call, started dressing. "You want to come to the bypass with me?"

Oliver nodded.

"Come on, then. After we've rounded him up, we need to go back to the station. Someone will be alerting the Spanish police about Gideon Davis, but I've got a shitload of interviewing to do—child suspects coming out of my arse—and too many things to get sorted. Let's wrap this fucking thing up. It feels like it's been going on for days."

* * * *

In the murky light that was pre-dawn, Langham drew the car up to the kerb behind a string of police cars. Coppers were strategically placed along the top of the bypass and at either end of the square tunnel below. Had they been instructed to wait for Langham before they acted, or had another detective or senior officer gone down the muddy incline and discovered the killer there? Maybe the man licking blood from his hands had drawn a weapon, holding up his arrest.

Oliver followed Langham to a sergeant standing on the rise and asked, "He been arrested?"

"No. He's asleep. Thought we'd better wait for you. Knew you were coming, see."

"Right." Langham shook his head, his thoughts clear on his face—'Doesn't anything get done around here without me being involved?'

All right, Oliver could see his point—to a degree—but this case was so far-reaching, too much for Langham to handle alone or with a small team, and other officers *had* been delegated jobs. Hundreds of coppers were working this case, if Oliver was any good at guessing.

As they walked away from the sergeant and down the slope, Oliver said, "Maybe they thought, because this is supposedly the last drugged-up killer out there, you'd want to be the one who brought him in."

Langham slipped on a particularly wet sheet of mud and nearly went down on his arse. "Yeah," he said over his shoulder. "But fucking hell, what if I don't want to be the one?"

"It's your job to be the one," Oliver said, nearly slipping on the same patch of mud even though he'd braced himself not to. "Like it appears to be my job lately to listen to the dead and see scary fucking devils at the end of the bed. Not what I'd have chosen, but there you go."

They came to a stop on a path strewn with tiny pebbles, loose dirt and a smattering of refuse. A supermarket receipt fluttered by, the long trail of paper undulating like an eel. Someone either had a big fucking family to feed or had bought food for a party. The paper seemed to go on forever before it finally fucked off and disappeared inside the tunnel.

Oliver stared into it, stomach rolling as the reason they were actually here tiptoed through his mind. Beneath there, in the darkness and shadows, was a man fast asleep—asleep after butchering an innocent woman.

How do you sleep after something like that? How do you live with yourself?

Langham walked ahead, approaching the tunnel on near-silent feet. He stopped to whisper to a pair of officers situated to the side and out of sight of anyone inside, nodded then turned to face Oliver.

"Stay there." His eyes said it all—'I don't want you to get hurt, because we've got this thing…'

Oliver nodded, thinking, *Yep, we've got this thing, and it might all come to an end when you walk into that tunnel. He might turn violent. He might...might take you away from me.*

The darkness scoffed Langham and the other two officers whole, and Oliver could only hope it didn't chew them up and spit them right back out again. Despite the insanity of this case, this was the happiest Oliver had been in forever. To have what he wanted handed to him on a plate, only to have it ripped away now... Shit, fate wasn't that cruel, was it? He fought the urge to leg it after Langham, to be there to protect him if things turned violent, but stopped. His presence in that tunnel might put Langham off his game, cause more harm than good. Oliver would just have to wait it out.

He didn't have to wait long. Langham's echoic voice emanated from the pitch a few seconds after a flashlight blared to life, the beam illuminating what looked like a heap of clothing on the ground.

"Asleep? A-fucking-*sleep*? Who the hell checked this guy? It's obvious he's fucking dead!"

Without waiting for permission, Oliver sped into the tunnel, coming abreast of the three standing men and the one on the ground. He stared at the corpse, its face frozen in an expression of innocence, as though the blood covering his skin was just makeup, that it didn't belong to Sasha Morrison. Had the man, a vagrant by the look of him, been given the drugs on the street then told where he needed to go when the urge to kill took over him? Too many questions, ones he was thankful he didn't need to know the answers to in order to get on with his job. Not now they had everyone involved either apprehended, in their sights or dead—but then what about those who had taken the drug, the ones they didn't know about? Langham could deal with it—Oliver would just be there to listen if his man felt the need to share.

He wanted to reach up, close the inches between them and hold Langham's hand, to give comfort to a detective who showed obvious signs of thinking his teammates were incompetent at times. Could Oliver do this...this job on a more permanent basis? He was momentarily startled by the thought but acknowledged that he wanted to be near Langham as much as possible, not just when the dead called. Was there some kind of title he could be given, other than informant, civilian help, that meant he could get regular pay, work side by side with the detective?

He hoped so. Despite the bone-weary tiredness it would bring when cases meant working for twenty-four hours or more in one go, despite people realising they were in a relationship that went beyond detective and his informant, despite every fucking damn thing, he hoped so.

Chapter Seventeen

Something Oliver had learnt early on in life was, despite wanting something so bad and praying for it, you sometimes never got it. Langham's request to have him as a permanent police partner of sorts was rejected. It had to be really, didn't it? Oliver had no formal police training, didn't get hunches or have any desire to actually *be* a copper—it wasn't in his blood, wasn't the thing that shoved him out of bed in the morning, ready to wade through another case, another day full of sick people with no regard for others, catching them and making sure they had a stint behind bars.

Perhaps the fact that the dead hadn't contacted him lately was a godsend. After the Sugar Strand case had finally ended, Gideon Davis apprehended after months of being watched, months of painstaking investigations to find evidence that had actually led the authorities to solid evidence that he was the mastermind behind it, Oliver was shattered for days. Knackered beyond description.

No spirits had contacted him since, and he wondered if he'd secured the cocoon a little too tight, making it so even the good ones couldn't come knocking. With his sleep no longer interrupted by death's call, he spent his days well rested and alert. He left his old job, wanting something new to do, and started a part-time position as an editor's assistant for the local rag—tea-making boy, more like—his boss agreeing that if Oliver was needed by the police in future, he could go on a moment's notice and also on the proviso that he gave reporters inside information on any high-profile cases he worked on. He'd checked with Langham on that, fucked if he wanted to get him into trouble for leaking anything he shouldn't. Langham had said he would give Oliver as much information as he could without compromising the investigations. Oliver's boss had been content with that.

So, all round, everything had worked out pretty well, although Oliver had a hard time keeping the images of the Sugar Strand case out of his head. Even though he'd told himself he didn't need answers, he apparently did. His subconscious asked for them when he slept, making him wake in a sweat, streams of queries flapping through his mind like that damn supermarket receipt he'd seen. There were too many victims, that was it. Too many bodies had stacked up, all owing to an arsehole named Gideon Davis, who wasn't spilling the beans on anything he'd done or why.

Before all this shit, Oliver had only had to deal with one dead body at a time — that of the spirit who contacted him — and that was hard enough. If a dead person did manage to get a hold of him again in the future, he hoped it would be like it had always been. Just one.

He sat in the police station's public waiting area, legs open, hands between his knees, gaze fixed firmly on the needs-a-damn-good-wash linoleum. Langham would be finishing work soon — five minutes max he'd said about half an hour ago — and they had a table booked at Grisotto's, some new Italian place in the city. He glanced up, watched those behind the glass pane of the front desk milling about, some on phones, some with their heads bent over paperwork, bored with the sight.

Lowering his head again, he watched an ant scurrying from beneath one of his boots towards the wall his chair was backed against, smiling wryly because even the insect had a mission. All he seemed good for nowadays was making tea with four sugars, filing old news stories and listening to his boss waffle on about needing new and exciting leads, nudge-nudge, wink-wink, get the dead to speak to you, boy. Oliver sighed every time, explained he couldn't just summon the dead people whenever he bloody felt like it and grimaced at the look of disbelief on his boss's face.

He admitted he felt lost without the dead. Yes, when they'd contacted him in the past it had sometimes been a bind, too much for him to handle, but their silence, their utter, deafening silence was worse. It made him feel useless, like he had no purpose. Langham assured Oliver he was needed—*'By me, man, isn't that enough?'*—and Oliver had gone on to explain that, although it should have been, it wasn't. Didn't Langham understand, what with his own job, his own desire to rid the streets of the filth that walked upon them, that a man sometimes needed a calling in order to feel truly whole? Oliver would love to say Langham was all he needed in life, but he'd be lying if he did.

And at the same time, it hurt, and he felt guilty that he wanted more.

The swoosh of the door leading to the innards of the police station had Oliver lifting his head, hope swimming through him that he'd see Langham breezing through the doorway. He didn't. Another officer swept by, oblivious to Oliver sitting there like a lost soul, waiting for his buoy to float by so he could hang onto it and feel *necessary*.

A policeman behind the desk tapped on the glass partition. "Langham's caught up in some last minute things. Said he'll meet you at home in about an hour."

So maybe they wouldn't be going to the restaurant, then. And home? Which one? Oliver's or Langham's? He didn't know but stood, sliding his hand into his pocket to finger the key to Langham's. He'd go there, hope he'd picked the right place. This past month he'd been to Langham's more than his own gaff and, as he pushed open the station's main door and walked out onto the street, he wondered whether they had some unspoken agreement that Oliver should live there. He wished he could bring the subject up—paying rent on his flat when he didn't spend much time there seemed stupid—but as Langham hadn't said anything about it, Oliver thought it best to keep his mouth shut.

After all, he didn't fancy putting Langham in the awkward position of having to tell Oliver he wasn't ready for that shit, that they'd only officially been a couple for a short while. Even though it had been months and the longest time Oliver had been with anyone.

He didn't fancy rejection.

On the walk 'home', he thought about the drugged kids, how they'd been reunited with their parents once they'd been given the all-clear by doctors and the police. They could hardly be charged for something they hadn't been aware they'd done. None of them remembered their acts or who had given them the drugs—none except Glenn Close, now living with a kind set of foster parents who gave her the life the girl should have had right from the start. If anything good had come out of that whole sorry mess, it had been that. She was young enough that the horrors could become a distant memory if enough good times eclipsed the bad.

He wandered along, feet knowing where to go. Good job, really, because his mind wasn't on the route he was taking, was it? As he rounded the corner into Langham's street, a cat zipped out of a bush, streaking across his path with a glance over its shoulder that brought a shiver-inducing thought to mind. Those creepy eyes, they'd never been explained. The kids had them, Alex Reynolds had them and he'd bet his next wage packet that the tramp under the bypass had them when he'd been alive. There was more to those eyes, Oliver knew it.

And they weren't anything to do with drugs.

Yeah, he knew how stupid that sounded, how fucking ridiculous that he entertained the idea that demons inhabited those people while they were under the influence, how no one wanted to acknowledge that the eyes were even a problem, a mystery that needed solving. And if he hadn't seen a demon with those eyes himself, he wouldn't have believed it either.

He sighed, walking into Langham's place. The scent of a good old British breakfast, stale now that hours had passed since it was cooked, welcomed him in. As oily as it smelt, he relished it—relished any scent to do with Langham, if he were honest—and closed the front door on a world gone crazy, the people out there, it seemed, all having something to do.

All except him.

Another sigh came out, and he shirked his shoulders and told himself not to be so bloody grim. He had a good man in his life, had a job, *two* roofs over his head. What was his problem? He walked down the short, no-room-to-swing-a-cat hallway then into the living room, where he slumped down onto the sofa, a beige velour thing that squeaked with every movement. He rested his head back and closed his eyes, wondering if a court date had been settled yet for Gideon Davis. For the first time, he wanted to follow up on the bad guy, visit the public gallery and see how things went after people had been caught. Maybe he only wanted to do that because it would mean seeing Langham take the stand, giving him time to study the man without feeling self-conscious. The only time he got to do that comfortably was when the detective slept, and, nine times out of ten, Oliver was so tired from a good fucking he ended up falling asleep mid-gaze.

He sat like that for a long time, opening his eyes when a key scraped in the lock, his belly clenching at the sound. He sat more upright, feeling a stupid wanker for staring at the doorway, probably with a longing expression on his face, fit for a schoolboy with a deep and searing crush. He had that crush all right, had it bad, and when Langham walked into the room, keys dangling from one finger, his hair dishevelled from having his hand go through it one time too many, Oliver had to stifle a whimper.

Oliver stood, sucking in the detective's weary countenance, the dark circles beneath his eyes. He didn't know what the man was working on at the moment, but it seemed to be taking its toll.

"You need rest," Oliver said, wiping out the space

between them and running his palm down Langham's face. "Shall we forget going to the restaurant?"

"Fuck, no." Langham raised his hand, covered Oliver's with it. "It's the weekend. Time for us."

Oliver laughed. "Criminals don't stop on weekends. You usually get called in."

"Not this time. That's why I'm late. Finished up my own case, laid the groundwork for a new one that came in when I was meant to be leaving so no bastard will need me for the next two days. Sorry about leaving you in the foyer like that."

He appeared sheepish, looked guilty.

"Hey, that's the way of your job. I know that." Oliver leaned his forehead against Langham's.

"Yeah, but—"

"Not discussing it. Been through this before." Oliver smiled, brushed his lips over the detective's, then stepped back. "Dinner. Back here. Bed."

"Sounds promising."

"It could be."

They left the flat after taking quick showers, the back of the cab they'd hired stinking of fish and chips and the hint of dried piss. Over dinner—some new-fangled pasta dish that tasted of too much cream and not enough garlic— they nattered about their days. Langham relaxed as the evening progressed, his shoulders a little less rigid, his jaw a little less set. Oliver liked to think he alone had done that, but wasn't vain enough not to realise the wine, the calm atmosphere and not being at work had played a major part.

As they finished up their dessert—oddly for an Italian restaurant, a very British treacle pudding and thick custard—Langham laid his spoon in his empty bowl and stared across the table at Oliver.

"This your place, my place thing," Langham said.

Oliver tensed, waiting for the words he'd dreaded since their relationship had started. He was at Langham's too much. Langham needed space. It was going too fast. They weren't as compatible as Oliver had thought…

"Yes?" he said, annoyed to hell and back that it had come out more of a squeak than a proper word.

"It's stupid."

Langham lifted his wine glass, sipped, eyed Oliver over the rim. Condensation dribbled onto his fingers, and Oliver wanted to stand up, lean over the table and lick it off. He couldn't, though. He wasn't sure a suddenly hard cock tenting his jeans was something other diners would appreciate.

"Oh right," Oliver said, fighting with his lust, telling his cock to soften. And *'It's stupid.' What the fuck does he mean by that?* Insecurity rose up in him, did a grand job of deflating his dick. "So, uh… Yeah, okay, I'll stay at mine all week. Some weekends. I'll come over when you ask, not just turn up. Sorry about that. Took it for granted you wanted me over all the time. Thought—"

"I do."

"Do what?"

"Want you over all the time."

"What?"

"You gone deaf?"

"No, but—"

"So what d'you think?"

"Of…?" Oliver didn't dare believe Langham was offering for him to move in. Shit like this didn't happen to him, did it? He'd expected their relationship to last a while then fizzle out, despite Langham saying otherwise, because shit, who wanted a freak like him around forever?

"Oliver… Come on, man. You're not stupid. Do I have to spell it out?"

Langham grinned, took another sip of wine, then placed the glass on the table. He waited for Oliver to respond, but Oliver couldn't. Hope was a dangerous thing. It made him think his dreams were within reach then snatched them back, breaking his heart. A few pulse beats thudded away the time, time that seemed suspended, everything around

Oliver fading so only him, Langham and the table existed.

"So I *do* need to spell it out." Langham's foot met Oliver's under the table. "I want you at mine all the time. Unless you want to keep your flat going. Might not want what I want." He paused, gave Oliver a questioning stare. "Might not want to live with me without the safety net of your place behind you. I understand that. I get it. Really."

Oliver couldn't form the words to respond.

Langham's face clouded. He'd got the wrong end of the stick with Oliver's silence. Shit. Oliver opened his mouth to say the words building up in his throat, but the bastards wouldn't come out. He floundered, trying to show Langham with his eyes that yes, fucking *yes* he wanted the same as him.

"We're still feeling one another out," Langham said, shifting nervously in his seat and taking hold of the wine glass stem, turning the glass around and around, the contents slopping about. He studied the glass, colour rising in his cheeks, far from the in-control man he usually was. "Just that, I thought we *had* this thing, know what I mean? I feel it, really fucking feel it, but I understand, really do. I'll leave it. We'll leave it. You just tell me when, or if, you want to move in, yeah? I mean—"

"Shut the fuck up." All right, it wasn't what Oliver had intended to say, but the words had the effect he'd been after. To make Langham stop talking. To make it so he wasn't baring his soul in front of other people. To make that grief-stricken look on his face go away. "I want it. Fuck, I want it. I was just… I didn't think you did, didn't think I'd be so lucky, that we'd even get this far, and you said what you said just then, and I shit myself, yeah? Fucking shit myself. Thought you were going to say…" Tears burned the backs of his eyes, and he ground his teeth together. If anyone else saw the tears fall, anyone but Langham, it would taint this moment.

Don't cry. Just don't bloody cry, you wanker.

Langham looked up. "Shit, you're struggling not to cr—"

He moved to get up, concern written all over him.

Oliver raised a hand, palm facing Langham. "Don't. It'll make me...fuck, it'll set me off. I can't...don't want to cry. Promised myself I wouldn't once I left home. Can't..."

Langham stood. "Get up. We're leaving."

Oliver rose, glancing about, disoriented as the rest of the room came into focus, bleeding around him like a lacerated wound, alien in the circumstances. They shouldn't be here like this. They should have talked about it in private, where Oliver could grip Langham by his upper arms and shove him onto the bed, demand that he fill his arse and ride him hard. He'd grown more confident in the bedroom over time, but tonight, with Langham asking him to move in... Damn, every bit of shyness he'd still harboured over the months vanished, replaced by an all-consuming need that drove him to whip out his wallet, throw cash down on the table and lead the way outside.

The cab ride home was fraught with sexual tension, neither one of them touching or looking at the other. The journey took too long, Oliver burning with an incessant urge to reach out and pull Langham's cock free of his jeans, suck him until he came down his throat. But he couldn't, didn't, and instead let the thought spread from his head and into his body that, well, what did you know, sometimes praying *did* work.

Chapter Eighteen

They clattered into Langham's, trying to fit through the doorway at the same time, Langham shutting the door behind them with his foot. The bedroom seemed too far away for Oliver, so he threaded his arms around Langham's waist and drew him close. Their mouths clashed, resulting in a kiss that tasted faintly of their meal but heavily of Langham's unique flavour. Oliver's cock strained, pushing so hard against his jeans he thought it might burst with his want to have it freed. Touched. Sucked.

It was as though Oliver couldn't kiss him hard or fast enough to convey what he felt inside, a body-filling euphoria that shit, he would be calling this place home, that he had arrived where he'd longed to be, in a more permanent relationship with a man he'd only dreamt of having in his life like this. He let his hands do what they would, let himself stop over-thinking what he should do next and just went with what felt right. He wanted to show more dominance, to have a more equal balance between them, to give Langham a break from always being the one to initiate or bring about what happened when they fucked.

He smoothed his hands back around to Langham's front, pushing them up to investigate the shape of hard chest and rigid nipples that stood to high little points beneath the shirt he wanted to rip off. Fingertips reaching the top button, Oliver kissed on and undid them one by one, skin brushing Langham's every so often, a burn of sexual electricity bolting through him every time. He drew the shirt off, letting it fall where it had a mind, and ran his hands over the exposed, heat-riddled skin of belly, chest then shoulders. Langham groaned, moving his hands with urgency to Oliver's zipper, fumbling with fingers that were usually so adept.

Had he taken Langham off guard with his orchestrating? Sent him a little off-kilter that Oliver appeared to be calling the shots? He wondered whether Langham would fight to get control back or if he'd allow him to continue. Oliver had to admit the thrill running through him at the thought of a battle was a welcome and damn pleasing sensation. He'd gained a sense of security with Langham offering to share his home, had felt the uncertainty melt away on the journey back here. He'd never thought they'd reach this point – had hoped for it more times than he could count – but no, he'd never thought they'd actually be here, now, like this.

"I fucking want you so bad," Oliver said as he broke his mouth away, coasting his lips to an earlobe, sucking it into his mouth and swirling his tongue around it.

Langham groaned again, all throaty and coated with lust, the reverberation of sound humming through that lobe and onto Oliver's tongue.

"You've got me," Langham said, "for as long as you want me."

Hands – it seemed they both owned more than a pair each as they stood there touching, breaths uneven. Oliver's cock strained again as Langham streaked his tongue tip up and down Oliver's neck. That was unfair. That action always undid him, bringing on shivers that spread out everywhere he could feel. Always made him want to give in and let Langham do whatever the fuck he liked for however long.

Oliver stepped back, breaking body contact completely, and stared at Langham. He stared back, a blush on his cheeks, his lips plump from kissing. He looked as though he was working out whether to make the next move or not. Whether it was Oliver's turn to take the lead. Whether finding out where Oliver would take them would be as exciting as him being dominant.

"Bedroom," Oliver said, the word full of breath and not

much bluster, even though he'd tried to inject a commanding edge. *Do it. Just tell it like it is, how it's going to be tonight.* "Get in there and get undressed. Wait on the bed."

Langham raised both eyebrows, his mouth hinting at a smile, lips then parting to release words Oliver assumed were bursting to come out. But he didn't say a word, just eyed Oliver for enough seconds to make him wonder if he'd be able to carry this through.

"Go on!" Oliver said, chest heaving as adrenaline began a speeding search-and-find through his body, seeking every part of him with intent to either make him wither under that stare or grow bolder.

Langham walked away, out of Oliver's peripheral vision. He didn't dare look to see if the man had gone in the direction of the bedroom, whether his command had actually been obeyed. He just hoped it had, because if it hadn't, he'd feel and look all kinds of fool. Waiting a few beats, Oliver undressed, leaving his clothes where they landed. He took a deep breath to combat the surging excitement, nerve endings pinging and sparking. Without a doubt, this was the boldest thing he had ever done with a man, taking control like this. It wasn't as alien as he'd feared when imagining it, kind of fitted like it was a piece of him that had always been there but he'd been unable to find.

After another huge breath, he walked to the bedroom doorway, keeping his gaze steady, right in front of him and not on the floor. The bed stood opposite, and Langham had propped himself up on it, pillows behind his back and head. Relief poured into Oliver, jiving with the frazzled nerves and adrenaline, and he swayed a little, reaching out to steady himself with one hand on the doorframe.

"You look good standing there like that," Langham said, studying Oliver's mid-section with greedy eyes. "I could just get up and lick you all over. Every damn inch."

Oliver held back a gasp. Langham wasn't playing fair, but that was to be expected. He was testing him, gently pushing to see if Oliver could handle what he'd started. It was a good thing, that. Oliver gathered his mettle, absolutely determined not to allow Langham the upper hand, the ability to have him caving under pressure, Langham retaking the dominant role. Oh, Oliver loved the way Langham knew what was what, all right, knew exactly how to get him off, but over the months he'd wondered just how it felt to give in to what his heart and body directed instead of being subservient and going with the flow.

Langham's cock, hard and ready, twitched, and Oliver had to stop himself hurtling onto the bed and sucking that dick right to the back of his throat. He huffed out a chuckle at having denied himself what he wanted. Hadn't he just wondered what it would be like to act on his thoughts as they came instead of giving them time to become comfortable in his mind?

He pushed off the doorframe, strode the short distance to the foot of the bed, then climbed on, all the while maintaining eye contact. Straddling Langham's legs and lowering his arse to settle on Langham's knees, Oliver slid one hand up the mattress to where their lube waited. Another thrill went through him that Langham had placed it there, appeared more than ready for his reins to be used by Oliver. Taking the lube in hand, Oliver sat upright again, still staring into Langham's eyes, and slowly unscrewed the lid. He cursed at his shaking hands, at his heart rate soaring as his mind raced with the knowledge that he'd better have the courage to see this through right until the end or he'd end up with egg on his heat-soaked face.

Squirting lube into his palm, he curled his hand around Langham's cock, drawing upwards then smothering it all over with fluid. Langham's cock vein thudded against Oliver's skin, the shaft pulsing, and he brushed his thumb over the tip, unsure whether lube or pre-cum was the source of the extra wetness there.

"You enjoying that?" Langham asked, hands flat on the bed beside him. "You loving the way it feels?"

"Are you?"

"Fuck, yeah."

Two words. That was all Langham had to say to make Oliver turn the man's hand over and squeeze a glob of lube onto his fingertips. Oliver released Langham's cock and repositioned himself, still straddling, facing the door with his legs spread wider than before, his arsehole on show within Langham's reach.

"Finger-fuck me," Oliver said, pleased with the way the words had come out—an order with a razor edge that wasn't quite sharp enough to cut.

He expected Langham to tease, to make him wait, and the immediate pressure at his arsehole surprised him. He relaxed his hole, a finger sliding in without effort, the tip brushing his prostate with enough force to elicit a gasp but not enough to make a groan. He reared back, pushing into that finger, wanting more.

"Another," he said.

Oliver looked into space, seeing nothing but the image of how Langham might appear if he turned around to check. Smile on his lips. One eyebrow raised. Eyes wide with his surprise. Was he licking his lips? Was his heart pattering at the same speed as Oliver's?

Langham withdrew his finger then pushed up with two, the extra thickness a glorious burn on Oliver's rim. He surged back again, seating the fingers as far as they would go, feeling knuckles against the cleft. Langham scissored his fingers, widening then closing, loosening Oliver's channel and easing away the burn as his tight pucker loosened. He was almost ready, he knew that—ready to take more fingers or Langham's cock. Oliver waited while Langham played, closed his eyes to better feel the emotion and pleasure rippling through him.

God, that man knew how to work an arse.

Oliver's balls retracted as Langham began an incessant, mind-and-cock-numbing set of strokes on Oliver's prostate. He'd shoot if he didn't regain control, if he let himself be carried away by the moment. With a touch of regret, he moved forward, fingers leaving him with a soft squelch of lube. That sound turned him on even more, and he retook his former position, although this time settled his arse on Langham's belly, the man's cock resting in Oliver's crease. Placing his hands on Langham's chest, he looked down at him while lifting up slowly until Langham's cock slid down his cleft and the head came to rest at his entrance. Without warning or saying a word, his breaths hitching and excitement building, Oliver sank down.

He tried not to close his eyes as Langham's cock eased inside, but with it halfway there he couldn't resist. In the darkness behind his closed lids, he could better feel the stretch, concentrate fully on being filled so wholly. He released a moan, long and drawn out, and clutched at Langham's chest. He realised then that Langham wasn't touching him, and he opened his eyes.

Langham had his closed, and he gripped the sheets in tight fists, teeth biting down on his lower lip. His chest inflated and deflated with such speed it told Oliver his lover was finding it difficult to control his emotions.

"Open your eyes and touch my cock," Oliver said, his stomach bunching, balls doing the same. "Put lube on my dick and enjoy what it feels like all wet."

Langham opened his eyes, one fist unclenching, hand then patting the bed in search of the tube. He found it, squirting liquid onto Oliver's cock, which jolted at the coldness even though he'd been expecting it. With a hot hand, Langham grasped him at the same time that Oliver sank down as far as he could go, and he thought for a split second it would be all over too soon.

He wasn't wrong. The newness of command, the fullness in his arse and that hand gliding wetly up and down his cock along with Langham groaning and fighting to keep his eyes open proved too much for Oliver to handle. A forceful throb in his balls travelled to the base of his dick, pounding without mercy. It was going to spread right up his length, and there would be no stopping the cum.

"Ah, shit. It's too late, I can't stop it," he said, lifting up then shoving back down on Langham's cock.

He rose and fell again, in time with Langham's hand, and a blast of euphoria swept through him, swiftly followed by a series of cum-shots jetting out of him. He scrunched his eyes shut, listening to his heavy breathing, Langham's heavy breathing and the strangled noises coming out of his lover. They served to heighten his experience, to force even more cum past his cock hole. It was agony yet wonderful, too many things happening at once. His arse channel exploding with bliss and burn, Langham's cock exploding with an orgasm that jolted his hips and thrust his dick deeper.

The next few seconds passed with Oliver's sight blurred and his mind off in some place he couldn't define. Some other world where nothing existed except him slowing on Langham, the detective reaching out to smooth his hands over Oliver's shoulders and down his arms and the feeling that he wished this moment would stretch on forever. One massive yawn of time that had no end, where real life didn't exist. No spirits, no cases, nothing.

As is usual, though, reality made its appearance known with a bone-jarring thump as the sound of a police siren wailed, one that belonged to a police vehicle that screeched down the street right outside. He sighed, lifted from Langham and immediately nestled beside him, ignoring the remains of the siren echoing through his mind. His head, resting on Langham's chest, rose and fell with the man's breathing, and Langham held him close with one arm about his back, linking his fingers to form a tight embrace.

This was the life, wasn't it? One Oliver had wanted, one he would fight to keep. Being in bed with Langham like this, as though he had the real right to be here, was the ultimate dream come true.

"We've got this thing, haven't we?" Oliver murmured. "A real thing?"

"Too fucking right." Langham squeezed him tighter, closer.

Tired out from their fuck, the alcohol and the sheer enormity of emotions he'd been dealing with tonight, Oliver felt sleep's fingers caressing him. He smiled, drifting on a current of security, of knowing that no matter what life threw at him now, he could cope with anything if his man was by his side.

As he reached the point where he'd drop off any second, Oliver jolted. Whispers, so very faint, filled his mind, growing louder by the second.

"Help me. Please! Oh, God, please help me…"

He shot upright, wide awake, adrenaline speeding through him.

"What the fuck?" Langham said, sitting up himself. He looked at Oliver. "Oh, shit. Not tonight. Please don't say someone's got hold of you tonight."

Oliver held up one hand. "Who are you, man? What's happened?"

"I'm floating. Can see myself down there. Some guy, he's… Oh my God. He's –"

"He's what? Where are you?" *Please answer me. Please…*

Langham's phone rang. Oliver sighed at the lost connection between him and the spirit, getting out of bed to have a very quick shower then dress. Under the hot spray, Oliver watched an image form in his mind, of a derelict warehouse on the outskirts of the city. He rinsed off and dried as fast as he could, racing out of the bathroom and back into the bedroom.

"The warehouses!" they both said at the same time, Langham snapping his phone shut.

Langham closed his eyes briefly then opened them with a nod. "So we have the same case then. That's what the sirens were about just now. Guy murdered. It's apparently a messy one."

"Aren't they all, in one way or another?" Oliver said, throwing Langham some clean clothes from his closet.

Their closet now.

186

VOICES

Oliver knows this is the first of many murders, and he's dreading the bodies piling up

SARAH MASTERS
WANTING

Wanting

Excerpt

Chapter One

Oliver Banks took a deep breath. The call from a dead male to the warehouse had been the first time he'd been contacted in months. He'd been nostalgic from lack of chatter from spirits, even though it took him to their death sites and he saw things most people couldn't even imagine seeing. All his life—as far back as he could remember anyway—he'd heard them, been called a weirdo by his parents, leaving home when the family taunts had finally got to be too much. He'd made it work for him, though, even assisted the police on cases, the Force finally accepting he wasn't involved in the murders, that he really did hear ghosts.

And hearing them breaks my bloody heart sometimes.

The air was hot. Stood to reason, what with it being the wrong side of winter, summer at its finest this year with temperatures well into the nineties. But the heat was different in here, different to what it was outside or at home. Like someone had a bonfire going, a huge, raging one, relentless heat coming off it, enough to sear your eyebrows. Oliver glanced around, past the police strolling the vicinity with their diligent, looking-for-clues paces. He eyed the forensic techs doing their thing in bootied feet and white paper suits, their hands covered in creamy latex that made them appear alien. He didn't see any reason for the heat, though. No fires on the walls, their orange-bar stripes belting out warmth, the image reminding him of the electric fire in the living room of his childhood. No new-fangled halogens, rectangles of bright yellowy orange that not only served as heaters but damn good sources of light that hurt the eyes if you stared at them too long.

Why the hell am I so hot then?

Sweat dribbled down his back, spread out over his armpits. He was uncomfortable in the extreme—and not just because he was so hot. Something very wrong had gone on here—something he sensed was more shocking than anything he'd dealt with before. He lifted his arms, put his hands on his hips casually, wondering, then not caring whether he had wet patches on his T-shirt. That kind of thing didn't matter in situations like this. The small stuff paled into insignificance by death. The everyday worries of how good you looked, if your breath stank and whether your hair needed washing just didn't figure for those called out to deal with the aftermath of some nutter's handiwork. Situations like this made him realise how insignificant his problems were. Quite simply, they didn't matter when compared to the fear the killer had inspired in his victim.

What must it be like to know you're at the end of your life? What the bloody hell goes through your mind?

He stared at the corpse. Young bloke in his twenties, Oliver guessed. Christ, what a waste. He'd only just begun living really, possibly leaving home, branching out on his own. Did his parents even know where he was? How he'd ended up? Oliver imagined them going about their day-to-day business, thinking their son was at work, maybe, when in reality... He didn't envy whoever had to tell them that their baby wasn't coming back.

It might even be Langham who gets that job. And I might have to go with him.

Oliver sighed. This man would have been good-looking in life, he reckoned. In death, though, he didn't look so good, but then who did? Even those who passed in their sleep—nothing untoward going on here, folks, move along please—tended to bloat, their orifices oozing fluid if their body hadn't been discovered in time for the nice mortician to do his thing. The things his lover, Langham, had seen. The bodies he'd been called out to view. Oliver wondered how the pair of them didn't constantly have nightmares.

Hank, the mortician, came to mind then, the man Oliver had had the pleasure of meeting a few months back. Pleasure seemed such an odd word given the circumstances, but Hank was a jolly man, probably having to be so due to the horrors he saw day in, day out. Hank would determine how this man had died, because although it seemed pretty obvious to Oliver that strangulation was the cause—the chain, look how tight that fucking chain is around his neck!—it might not be so cut-and-dried. He could have been killed first then strung up the way he had been—and Oliver knew this was a murder not a suicide. What the hell went through a killer's mind? Did they sit at home envisaging what they'd do to their victims? Write notes?

If he'd been told years ago he'd be standing in front of some poor, dead bastards on a regular basis, he'd have shit himself.

Funny how things turned out.

More books from
Sarah Masters

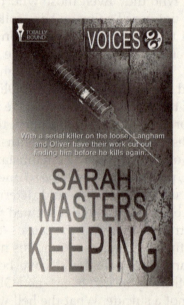

Book three in the Voices series

*With a serial killer on the loose, Langham and Oliver have
their work cut out finding him before he kills again…*

About the Author

Sarah Masters

Sarah Masters is a multi-published author in three pen names writing several genres. She lives with her husband, youngest daughter, and a cat in England. She writes at weekends and is a cover artist/head of art in her day job. In another life she was an editor. Her other pen names are Natalie Dae and Geraldine O'Hara.

Sarah also co-authors with Jaime Samms, and as Natalie Dae she co-authors with Lily Harlem under the name Harlem Dae.

Sarah Masters loves to hear from readers. You can find contact information, website details and an author profile page at https://www.pride-publishing.com/

PRI))E

PUBLISHING